The Orphans of
RASPAY

The Orphans of
RASPAY

A PENRIC & DESDEMONA
NOVELLA IN THE WORLD OF
THE FIVE GODS

Lois McMaster Bujold

SUBTERRANEAN PRESS 2020

First Hardcover Edition

ISBN
978-1-59606-972-5

Subterranean Press
PO Box 190106
Burton, MI 48519

subterraneanpress.com

Manufactured in the United States of America

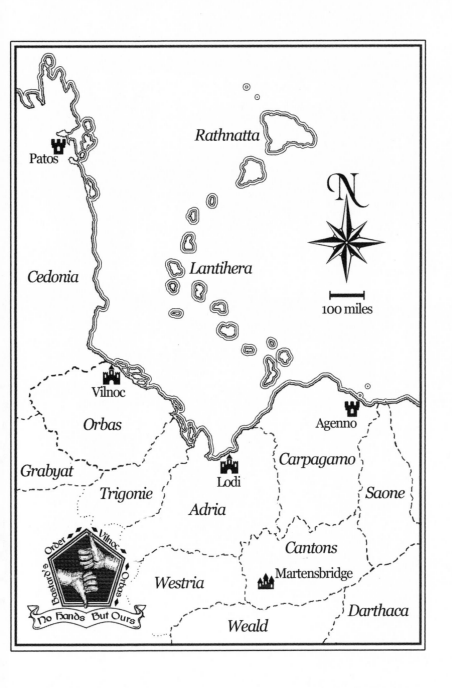

Patos

Rathnatta

Cedonia

Lantihera

N

100 miles

Vilnoc

Orbas

Agenno

Grabyat

Trigonie

Carpagamo

Saone

Lodi

Adria

Cantons

Vilnoc

Order

Bastard's

Orbas

No Hands But Ours

Westria

Martensbridge

Darthaca

Weald

*T*HE SICKENING *CRUNCH* threw Penric out of his coffin-sized bunk and onto the deck of his scarcely larger cabin, and from deep sleep into frantically confused consciousness in the same moment. Blackness all around him; he called up his dark-sight from his demon Desdemona without thought, though there was nothing new to see in this narrow space. Everything that could move had been tied down in the last day, as the ship had pitched and rolled its way through an unexpected tempest that had blown them, well, he hoped the crew knew where, because he certainly did not.

The horrible motions and the groaning of the ship's timbers had tamed, which explained how he'd finally fallen asleep despite his nausea and alarm. It did not explain the shouts and cries coming from outside, in a more terrified tenor than the workmanlike bellows of the crew manhandling the ship through the storm. Had they run onto rocks?

Des, what's happening out there?

Her reply was terse. *Pirates.*

In the middle of the night? ...How could two ships even *find* each other in such murk?

It's morning, she replied. *Apart from that, unhappy chance, I expect.*

Pirates were a known hazard all along the coasts and islands, but more to the north than the south where Pen's ship should have been, just a day or two out from Vilnoc and home. Curse it, he wanted to be *there*. Not dealing with *this*.

He was a Temple sorcerer, possessing the most potent chaos demon he knew of. Long before he'd stepped aboard this modest cargo carrier in Trigonie, he had imagined any number of clever magical defenses against such evil attacks, subtle enough not to reveal his nature and calling to the men on either vessel. He now realized that he had always pictured pirates happening on a bright afternoon, in quiet seas, with a good long time to see the villains *coming*.

Sorcerers, and the chaos demons that gave them their powers, were considered bad luck on a ship, and many captains would not take them aboard at all. Mild-mannered Temple scholar or no, Penric thus routinely traveled incognito when he was forced to take a sea passage. Pirates, he expected, would give even shorter shrift to the hazard of him: roughly the distance from the thwart to the heaving water.

Oh, yes, agreed Des grimly. Who, with her two centuries of experiences, knew the risks firsthand. Pen fought against the panicked memories flooding his mind from one of her unluckier prior possessors. He had plenty of current panic on his plate to attend to.

Because mixed among the voices crying in Adriac and Cedonian out there, he heard shouts in Roknari. Pen rubbed his sleep-numbed face and scrambled up, listening harder.

No seamen loved sorcerers, but the Roknari heretics, who abjured the fifth god Whom Penric served as a seminary-trained divine, considered all who worshipped Him an abomination, to be either forcibly converted to their foursquare faith, or inventively executed. Not that Pen *worshipped* his god exactly; their relationship was more complicated than that. Pirates, Pen tried to encourage himself, were unlikely to be passionate about the fine points of theology. On the other hand, they were a superstitious lot.

If there was anything more likely than his sorcery to result in him being summarily tossed overboard, with or without torture first—

Attempted torture, Des put in with a snarl.

—it was certainly Pen's calling as a divine of the white god. Both of which would be revealed by his possessions: the garb of his Order, his Temple braids, the letters and documents he carried, all packed away tight in a sealed chest stuffed under his bunk. Plus the three ancient scrolls he'd picked up in Trigonie, which he hadn't even had a chance to read through yet, let alone translate, of which pirates were unlikely to recognize the value at all. He shuddered.

Turning, he knocked open the tiny port at the back of his cabin in the stern of the ship, admitting a leaden illumination. He didn't think his shoulders would squeeze through, nor had he the least desire to anticipate their assailants' murderous actions by throwing *himself* overboard, but, holding his wooden case up to the aperture, he thought it just might fit. Still he hesitated.

Des, impatiently, ran a line of hot disorder around under the lid, sealing it more firmly. *It's more likely to float than we are. Get* rid *of it.*

Thuds like sledgehammer blows against his locked door made him flinch and shove it through. *Lord god Bastard, Fifth and White, if ever you loved me, let this find me again somehow.* More prayer than spell, surely. Too much noise to hear a splash, though the cries out on the ship were dying away.

Who had won? was a question answered by the brutish banging. As the door burst inward he turned and fell to his knees, something between supplication, surrender, and the thought that if the pirate came in swinging, his aim would be too high.

Pen blinked in the dingy gray light framing the hammerer's broad shoulders, and reminded himself that he could see out better than the man could see in. Confirmed at once when the pirate said, in a voice of surprise, "A woman?"

For once, Penric did not rush to correct this annoying misapprehension, though Des muttered, *Being female's not as much help as you'd think.* Electrum hair shining in a mussed queue, blue eyes, fine features, a lean build that might at a glance be mistaken for slender; the error had been made before. His pale coloration, common in the mountainous cantons where he'd been born, was rare here in the lands of Cedonia, Adria, and the Carpagamon islands surrounding this sea. In any case, the man did not at once try to bash in his blond head.

Which allowed Pen time to fling up his convincingly ink-stained hands and cry in common Adriac, "I'm a scribe!" The *Don't hurt me, I'm valuable! And harmless!* was implied, if the fellow wasn't too drunk on violence to care.

If he was, Pen readied a disabling attack on his nerves, regretting, not for the first time, the theological, no, divine proscription upon using Des's magic to kill. Directly. Not that it would help much even if Pen could slay them all, because then what? He was lost on the sea in a ship no single man, even a trained sailor, could manage by himself. If only he could stay alive until they reached some shore, although preferably not in the Roknar Archipelago, it would be a different tale.

...What a strange moment he had come to that he was *wishing* for slavers.

The hammer man grabbed him by the shoulder and dragged him through the cabin door and out onto the still-rolling deck, though waves were no longer washing up on it. As his knees scraped the boards, Pen was glad he'd worn tunic and trousers to bed, though he was sorry his feet were bare. The gloom of his cabin gave way to a steely dawn, the ashy lid of the clouds, directionless, matched by the slate of the sea. A second fellow leaned around his comrade to stare at their catch.

"No, it's a man," the door-breaker corrected himself, in a tone of disappointment. Pen kept his beseeching hands raised, hoping this discovery wouldn't just result in the hammer swinging around for a blow. "Of a sort."

"Father's balls and Mother's tits," the second man swore, rudely. In Adriac, they were both speaking an island dialect of Adriac, so where had those Roknari shouts come from? Penric's own ship's crew had mostly spoken Cedonian, and he wasn't hearing them anymore. "If that skinny arse was ten years younger, it'd fetch a *fortune*."

Twenty years, Pen thought irritably. It didn't take much of a stretch to manage an authentic quaver: "Spare my hands!" Along with eyesight, hands were a scribe's main tool and value. He wasn't going to even *suggest* his eyes.

"Hah. Behave, or we'll cut 'em off," the hammer man threatened, fulfilling Pen's assessment. He bent and undid Pen's belt, shoved the belt-knife sheath into his own trouser band, and efficiently used the leather strap to hitch Pen's wrists painfully behind his back. Pen barely mourned the loss of the knife, slim and sharp more for mending quills than sticking into people. Stripped naked, he'd still be the least disarmed man on this vessel.

Vessels, he emended, finally getting a chance to look around.

The pirate ship was smaller and slimmer than the cargo coaster, jammed up with its starboard bow grappled to the coaster's midships. One mast to their two, yet probably faster, given that most of the coaster's sails were lashed down to deal with the storm, its hull lumbering with a bulk lading of timber and cheap ceramics. Their attacker wasn't a military oarship, anyway, nor some government-appointed privateer. It had the grubby look of a typical all-trades Carpagamon-islands build, suitable for a bit of fishing, a bit of transport…a bit of opportunistic theft and lucrative kidnapping. Not the sort of arrogant venture that seized valuables from some rich merchanter, then sank the target and its passengers to be done with the trouble. Granted, such ships were much better defended. Pen found himself hoping for more-frugal pirates.

Still-wet blood smeared the damp deck here and there, but no dead bodies. Valueless corpses already stripped and tossed overboard? Up at the bow, the survivors of the crew, which by Des's headcount and to Pen's relief seemed to be most of them, were being shoved together and secured by a larger and presumably more vicious group of attackers.

His census was not done. Pen sighed inwardly and thought, *Des, Sight.*

A couple of fresh ghosts, still bearing the crisp if colorless forms of life and agitated by their deaths, whirled around the deck. Pen could not tell which sides they had been on. He mentally readied a prayer for their succor, though even as he watched one was drawn up and away to the *Elsewhere* by its god—the Father, Pen judged by a wintry tinge that he almost expected to trail a gust of snow in the damp, warm air. The other spirit seemed more lost.

The Bastard was, among many other things, the god of leftovers, last home to all the souls that no other of the Five would take. Criminals, execution-ers, orphans, whores, bastards, sorcerers, some artists and musicians, those with odd loves, and, yes, pirates. (On the whole, Pen much preferred to deal with pros-titutes, with whom he got along *fine.*) Theologically, a divine of the Bastard was obliged to care for them all. He didn't have to *like* them all, fortunately. Just fulfill his duties to them, if no one else could.

The dead could be sundered from the gods in two—no, three ways. A soul might refuse the union, through fear or hate or despair. Rarely, a soul might be so rank and spoiled from the sins of its life that even the Bastard wouldn't take it. Or a soul might become mazed in that brief liminal space between life and the life beyond: looking back too hard to look forward, disoriented and confused, or trapped by uncanny events—Penric had untangled a few of those, memorably.

There was nothing especially uncanny about this darting ghost. He seemed to be a bandy-legged youth, late teens or early twenties, wearing the memory of the clothes he'd just died in: a sailor's trousers and tunic that might have come from either crew. It was disorientation and despair that mired him here, in Pen's reasonably practiced diagnosis.

Pen was already on his knees, though his hands, tied behind his back, could not sign the tally of the gods. He could tap his fingers to his thumb, and did, mutely naming a deity for each digit. He dared not speak the prayers for the dead aloud, revealing his calling to his captors. But such eulogies were mainly for mourners. Silent speech would do for the gods. And for the dead.

The ghost drew near as he began to unwind the words in his head, his tongue moving behind closed lips. More a warm-up than anything else yet, till he could guess what this snag was. The boy just looked bewildered. Pen switched from Adriac to the Cedonian language and started again. Still no dice. The boy's attention tightened as it dawned on him that Pen was the only person here who could *see* him. Though Pen could not hear him; the bodiless mouth pushed no sounds through the air. But its shapings gave Pen the clue he sought.

Pen switched to Roknari. His Roknari accent was a little archaic, Des had informed him, though intelligible to those commanding either the high or the vile versions of the language. *Ah. He's a Roknari Quadrene.* Refused by the Father of Winter or the Son of Autumn, the preferred and expected gods, so presumably one of the pirates. *What are you?* the boy's wide eyes cried, taking in the peculiar spiritual aura of the blond stranger who held a demon. Which with Des, Pen knew, likely looked fathoms deep.

"If you were going to hold to your foursquare faith," Pen found himself whispering aloud, "you should have picked a different line of work. Or the other way around. Too late now. The white god invites you—though not for long."

Pen could feel, though not see, never see, that huge Presence, somewhere on the other side of the air. So could Des, for she retreated within him, muttering, *I wish at least you wouldn't* bait *Them.*

Not my doing, Des. Death opened a door to the gods as nothing else could—except for saints, Pen supposed, which he certainly was not. The gods in turn were the only force that could destroy chaos demons, once they had anchored themselves in some living being, hence Des's swallowed fear.

Sometimes, Des, I actually have to do the job I vowed to do. Though not for the Temple.

*Yes, yes...*she grumbled, but—valiantly, Pen thought—held her powers available to him in the teeth of this divine gale. She had grown worlds better at this in the thirteen years he'd held her. Confident in his protection?

"It will be all right," Pen told the boy, on exactly no evidence. Pen wasn't sure if staring fiercely at people until they believed him was a skill of divines or of dissemblers, or if there was a difference. Point was, someone who'd let other people tell him what to think all his young life might need permission to change even at the last gasp. And this one wasn't going to get more chances now to grow into his gods, was he? "It will be very well. Five gods bless you on your journey."

Do they? the distraught boy mouthed.

"Yes," said Pen. "Though only one holds out His hand, I promise His grip is sure, and will not drop you into any imagined hell."

Into strangeness, yes; Pen had seen hints enough of the strangeness of the world on the other side of reality. One of his seminary masters had argued that it was as impossible to truly grasp as for a child still in the womb to imagine its breathing life beyond the pains of birth. Pen still meditated occasionally and uneasily on that metaphor.

Pen wanted a year to instruct, to counter whatever lies the Quadrene teachers had instilled in the youth that were dividing him from his choosing-if-not-chosen god, but neither of them was going to get it. Yet…whatever Pen had so clumsily said and done, it must have been enough to tilt the necessary moment of assent, since ghost and Presence disappeared abruptly from his Sight.

Pen didn't even get a holy pat on the head for his pains. This wasn't saint-work. Pen hadn't, couldn't, channel a god; he was otherwise already inhabited.

Arguing with a human on the god's behalf, now, that he might do. He let the visions go with a huff of relief.

The respite was short-lived. He'd taken his attention away from the world of matter for a little too long. Evidently thinking his captive had been gibbering in hysteria, hammer-man slapped Pen's face, fortunately with his open hand and not his weapon—which in the seeping light turned out to be a rusty old Cedonian army-issue war hammer, Pen noted dizzily—and grabbed him by the scruff of his tunic to drag him along the deck. Pen let himself be dragged, trying to reorient himself.

"What have you got yourself there?" another rough voice asked.

"White rabbit." The grip shook Pen, cruelly amused. "Says he's a scribe. What d'you want done with him?"

"Could be a prize. Or dinner. Drop him in the small hold with the other virgins."

"Is that safe?"

A thick hand checked the security of Pen's looped belt, lifting his arms up in ways they weren't meant to bend. Pen yelped, wishing he were acting. "What's he going to do with his hands tied behind his back? We'll deal with him later."

Safe for who? Pen wondered as he was hoisted over the rail by his two finders and flung down onto the deck of the other ship. He had a quick, swinging impression of mast and boom, spars and ropes; then a heavy wooden lattice set in the deck was heaved out of the way, and he was chucked into a dark, square hole. Feet first, thankfully.

He plummeted only a little more than his own height, but without his arms for balance he landed crookedly and fell sideways to smack into a bulkhead, then flop to the floor. He lay for a moment catching his breath as the lattice thudded back into place overhead, a black weave set with graying squares. The dark smelled of old timber and tar, fish and rancid oil, spilled stale wine, with a more recent overlay of piss and sour vomit. He'd been in worse oubliettes, though not lately.

More importantly, he wasn't alone.

…Or less alone than he usually wasn't. He had only to want his dark-sight, and it was there, stripping away the shadow. *Thank you, Des.*

Any time. Her curiosity seemed equal to his own; her alarm, now their captors were out of hammer range and the soul-harvesting gods had decamped, less.

Grunting, Pen heaved himself upright and rested one shoulder against the bulkhead. In the corner of the space, as far from him as they could creep—which was only about six feet—two small figures cowered.

Oh. Children. Pen started to ease to the opposite corner, realized it was the designated chamber pot, and stayed where he was. Des, at his wisp of thought, unloosed the straps around his wrists, and he retrieved and redonned his belt. He propped his back against the wall more comfortably, stretching out his long legs, and took stock.

Two girls. Perhaps ten and eight? Sisters, possibly, though resemblances were hard to gauge from youth-rounded features. Their clothing was ordinary, calf-length tunics with dyed braided belt ties, simple but carefully sewn; little jackets, leather sandals. His summation of their medical state was reflexive, still hard to resist for all that he had disavowed the calling of physician. They were parched, bruised, tense, hungry; but without broken bones, cuts, or deeper hurts. *It could be worse.*

It still could.

Pen licked his own dry lips, gentled his voice. Tried Adriac. "Well, hello there, you two."

They flinched and clamped each other tighter, staring wildly at him.

Cedonian. "I won't hurt you." Still no help. He repeated his greeting in Darthacan, and then Ibran, which won a twitch. All right, one more...

"Hello, there." Adding the endings in high Roknari that suggested *teacher to student*, he continued, "My name is Master Penric. My rank is scribe. What are your names?"

Their frozen grips upon each other scarcely slackened, though as the silence stretched the older proffered, a bit convulsively, "I can write. A little."

A social effort? Claiming value for herself? In any case, the brave venture into speech should be rewarded. "That's very good."

Not to be outdone, the smaller one put in, "I can draw."

Sisters, no doubt of it. Pen's lips twitched up in a smile that wasn't even false. "So what should I call you?"

The older swallowed and said, "My name is Lencia Corva."

"I'm Seuka," said the younger, frowned, and added, "Corva."

Seuka was a Roknari name, Lencia was Ibran, and Corva... Corva was interesting. Their accents were revealing; not the pure Roknari of the Archipelago, but the melodious variant of the Roknari princedoms that capped the great peninsula of Ibra on its northern shore. The girls did manage the polite endings that placed Pen's claimed rank as higher than their own. A Roknari princeling would have addressed a scribe as a servant. Or, Pen was grimly reminded, as a slave.

In the growing light from the grating, Pen noted cropped brown curls on the older one's head; tighter, redder curls on the other's, their springy unruliness prisoned by a grubby ribbon at her nape. Lightish eyes on each, though he could not make out the color quite yet. Both skinny, but not starved despite recent hunger.

"Did the pirates get you, too?" asked Lencia.

"I'm afraid so." Pen leaned his head, which unsurprisingly ached, back against the wooden bulkhead. "I was sick from the storm, and then I was asleep. I was supposed to be sailing to Vilnoc in Orbas." He wondered if it would reassure them to mention the wife who awaited him there, with luck not-yet-anxiously. *No.* He would keep Nikys, and every other vulnerability, clutched tight to his chest for now. Though tossing out these little verbal breadcrumbs as though trying to attract birds seemed to be fruitful.

"We were going to find Papa in Lodi," said Lencia. "But then everything went wrong."

"He was *supposed* to be in Agenno, but he wasn't," said Seuka, sounding peeved.

Agenno was a major port on the coast of Carpagamo, near the border of Saone; about the halfway point in the eight hundred east-west miles that separated the Ibran peninsula and Lodi. These girls were farther from their birthplace than Pen was from his.

Hm, said Des. *A hundred years ago, 'Corva' was an Ibran nickname for a whore. Crow-girl. Not wholly rude. Doesn't exactly square with a papa. I suppose it could have become a surname since then...*

"Master Corva of Lodi, then?" Pen led on.

"No, our papa is Master Ubi Getaf," said Lencia, with earnest precision. "He's a merchant from Zagosur."

Which was the royal capital of Ibra, and its main entrepôt.

"Taspeig wrote to him after Mama died, but the letter just came back saying he'd gone trading to

Agenno. So Taspeig tried to take us there, but at the factor's post they said he'd gone on to Lodi, and she wouldn't go any farther."

Taspeig was another Roknari name, by derivation at least. "Was she a relative?"

Seuka shook her head, the wad of curls moving with it. "No, she was Mama's servant. We don't have any relatives. Mama said that's 'cause she was an orphan."

Pen had a distinct sense of his boots sinking into a bog, deeper and deeper.

"Papa gave Mama a little house in Raspay," Seuka went on. "I liked it there. We slept out on the porch above the back garden when it was hot. But the landlord said we couldn't stay there by ourselves without Mama."

Raspay was a modest port town in the princedom of Jokona, on the western side of the peninsula, right. A merchant based in Zagosur might easily make it the terminus of some personal coastal trade route. "Did your papa have no family in Zagosur?"

Lencia scowled. "Too much. He has a wife and children there. He wouldn't ever take us to meet them, and Mama said *she* didn't know, and we weren't to pester."

She being, presumably, the legitimate wife. Some such women were tolerant of husbandly by-blows. Most were not. So if not orphans outright, the sisters were half-orphans for certain; bastards by Ibran law, and by Jokonan as well if the second wife wasn't official.

And, of course, they were here. As he was. Was propinquity a theological hazard?

"So, Jokona," sighed Pen. "Are you Quadrenes or Quintarians?"

They tensed, looking anxiously at each other. "Which are you?" said Lencia after a cautious moment.

"Quintarian," said Pen firmly. "Very common in my country." Countries, he supposed. He had traveled far from the cold cantons in late years.

Two sets of narrow shoulders relaxed. "Papa is Quintarian," Lencia offered. "Mama said we could be Quintarian at home, but had to be Quadrene outside. So... I don't know...partly?"

Pen spared a moment of fresh loathing for the sectarian idiocy that made even children afraid.

Well. A trained divine and sorcerer seemed a generous gift to fellow wards of the white god, here in this hold. Though surely any other decent adult would have taken up responsibility for the helpless...

The gods are parsimonious, murmured Des, slyly quoting his own text back at him. A slight sense of preening.

So it seems. Just once, Pen thought glumly, he'd like to *get* an answer to prayers, instead of being *delivered* as one.

And where are we going now? If his bodiless demon had possessed any eyes but his own, Pen thought they'd be crinkled in amusement.

Lodi. Evidently. He could feel the new weight dropping onto his shoulders like baggage onto a packhorse. *Somehow.*

CLUNKS AND clanks vibrated through the bulkhead, and the thumps of footfalls. Calls in Adriac and Roknari filtered down through the grating— bellowed orders and acknowledgements, not screams. The ship surged sideways, evidently unmooring from the cargo coaster. Flapping canvas snapped taut, and the ship heeled in response.

Des, what can you make out? It was past time to take a wider survey of his situation and what resources he had.

They seem to have split their crew. Taking the coaster whole as a prize, I daresay. I imagine they will travel in convoy to whatever port they use to sell off their captives and goods.

Which port was an important question. In times of war, combatants on all sides would haul captured enemies home to be ransomed or enslaved, depending on their rank. But though conflict among the realms bounding this sea was endemic, Pen hadn't heard rumor of any open warfare this season. Their pirates seemed to be strictly a venture of commerce, homegrown.

The blend of languages in the crew was telling. Adriac-speaking Carpagamo wrestled with the Roknari for hegemony over the long chain of mountainous islands that ran north and swung around to the east, with a gap of open sea before the Archipelago proper. The islands closest to the mainland were held firmly by Carpagamo, though sometimes Adria or Darthaca muscled in. The islands at the looping tip were usually held by some Roknari prince. In between was a debatable stretch that went back and forth, or was left as a neutral buffer if times were peaceful. This mixed lot of sailors had to be from one of the often-brutalized buffer islands, and

Pen could only wish Quadrenes and Quintarians could be so cooperative for better ends.

Umelan, Desdemona's—eventual—sixth human possessor, had been a war victim, kidnapped from her Archipelago island home by a Darthacan military raid and sold south to Lodi. Continentals captured by the Roknari were sold north to the Archipelago. In both directions, the scheme worked the same way to tame captives, separating them from families, communities, languages and religions, dropping them down off-balance in strange friendless places. There they would have no choice but to cooperate in the theft of their labor, while working to scrape together what funds they could to buy their way out, or hope to be granted freedom as an act of charity by their bond-holders. Umelan had received such a boon in the will of Des's fifth possessor, the courtesan Mira of Lodi. The receipt of Mira's demon at her death had been less planned.

Umelan's experiences were a century out of date, and in general Pen did not enjoy dipping into her unhappy memories, or, worse, having them invade his dreams, but she was a resource of information better than any scroll. Place her in the plus column.

(A sour snort, he thought, from that one-twelfth layer of Desdemona that was Umelan. He mentally offered her a humble salute in return. She had, after all, gifted him with her language, for all that he had refined his command subsequently by his own studies.)

A buffer-island port would host small merchants and traders from all over, so captives might be sold either north or south. The coaster's men and Penric would be earmarked for north. It was a coin toss whether being enslaved on the galleys or in the mines was more lethal, but either was to be vigorously avoided. Female captives commonly were given over to the same domestic duties they would have been performing at home: spinning, weaving, gardening, cleaning, cooking, childcare. Childbearing. What fate was planned for these Jokonan girls was a puzzle, though the fact that they were being kept separate and relatively unharmed was probably not due to kindness.

In any case, the need to rid themselves quickly of their perishable prizes, plus the division of their crew, meant that the islander pirates would be heading straight for port. Pen could not hope for some new clash to turn out the other way and lead to his rescue.

"Is your papa a rich merchant?" he asked the Corva sisters. "Do you think he would ransom you, if word were taken to him in Lodi?" If Master Getaf was still in Lodi, among other uncertainties. But promise of a ransom greater than their sale price as slaves could be a major protection for them. Possibly safer than hooking up with a displaced sorcerer on the run.

They looked at each other in surprise, so this wasn't a thought they'd already had. Hm.

"I...maybe not *very* rich," said Lencia.

"He brought us presents," Seuka offered, in an equally hesitant tone.

And had housed a long-time mistress, but unless Master Getaf kept a family in every port, maybe just the one. Hold the ransom notion aside for now.

Trying to offload our baggage already? murmured Des.

Trying to think sensibly. This hasn't been a good morning.

I could sink this ship in five minutes.

I know you could. Please refrain, at least till we're on dry land. Pen considered this. *I might let you have it then.*

For a present? Des was amused, contemplating this chance at chaos.

You are not my mistress. Thankfully. For all that she was the permanent extra party in his marriage bed, and any other. Thank all the gods for tolerant, wise Nikys. He tried not to think too much about Nikys, because the worry would make him frantic and stupid.

There were enough other distractions. He cast a "Pardon me, please," over his shoulder at the girls, and turned to hunch over the latrine corner. Some seepage at the hold's seams had reduced the liquid level, which was why the pitching of the ship hadn't spread it all over the floor, but still, ugh. *Let's do something about this mess. What's underneath?*

...Bilges and ballast.

Too bad it wasn't pirate hammocks. *Open us some drainage. Quietly.*

Des applied some chaos, Penric supplied some order, or at least aim, and a ragged hole in the deck dropped out. Aware of his audience, he relieved himself as discreetly as he could.

Sanitation improved, he supposed the next problem he could actually address was clean drinking water. Which was a trivial task, except for the lack of a cup. With the air so damp he could spin water off his fingers, catching the trickle in his mouth or other receptacle, but that created the problem of concealing his magic from his hold-mates. He had no idea what wild tales they had imbibed about sorcerers in Quadrene lands, when Quintarians weren't much better informed, but there was a decided possibility that their first response to his gifts would be panic.

Are there other prisoners aboard? he asked Des.

The dizzying doubled vision of her demonic perceptions came to him as though they were his own, and Pen wondered if he would someday no longer be able tell them apart. The boundary between his will and her magic was already invisible whenever he was in too much of a hurry to take care to distinguish.

Another hold, aft, held half-a-dozen distressed people, some injured. Not from Pen's ship; aside from him, the captured crew had been kept aboard their own vessel. The pirate ship's own crew was scarcely more numerous than their prisoners at this point, though they must have started out with a crowd of rowdies to be sure of outnumbering their targets. His coaster would appear to have been the second ship seized on this venture, stretching the brigands' reserves.

"How long have you two been in here?" Pen asked the Corva sisters. "What ship were you on, and where was it taken? It couldn't have been a large one." Lions might bring down great oxen, but feral dogs had to scrape a living from rabbits, mice, and carrion.

Lencia shook her head. "Taspeig set us on a big ship at Agenno, that was supposed to go all the way to Lodi, but it had to put in at another port on account of woodworm. So we found a littler ship that was supposed to be going that way, that would take us on the promise that Papa would pay. Except some other passenger paid them to go north to some island first, and that's where the pirates came."

Opportunistic chance, or might that rich-seeming passenger have been a stalking horse, selecting a bite-sized target and leading it into ambush? If so, that was one clever son of a bitch Pen might attend to later himself, if he could.

"The captain fought, but he was killed"—Seuka shivered, looking sickened—"and the rest surrendered pretty quick."

"That was...six days ago?" said Lencia uncertainly, swallowing. "And then there was the storm. I don't know where we are now."

"You two have been having quite an adventure," said Pen, trying to sound friendly without encouraging the teary breakdown that evoking these memories threatened.

Lencia scowled. "I don't think I like adventure."

"I have to agree," said Pen, offering a wry grin. He rubbed his nape under his queue, rose, and stepped into the stretched blocks of sunlight now angling through the grid. The clouds were clearing, or else they had sailed out of their cover. The sisters both stared up at him, lips parting.

The easterly slant of the light shafts was obvious at this hour; the ship was therefore heading roughly north, allowances made for tacking against the wind or currents. Not a surprise. Pen tried shouting upward in common Adriac, "Hoi! We need some drinking water down here! And food!" As long as he was at it. "Hoi!" He would rather drink the remarkably pure water Des produced than anything that came out of a ship's cask, but it might come with a cup he could purloin, to share.

Pen hastily tucked his hands behind his back, as if still bound, when a face loomed at the grating. Its stubble might be on either a Carpagamon with a recent beard-trim or a Roknari who'd missed his chance to shave. The conundrum wasn't solved when the fellow merely grunted, but in a little while a stick of hard bread was dropped down through the grating, followed by a leather water bottle with, blessing, a wooden cup tied to it by a rawhide cord.

This was evidently the routine method for sustaining the prisoners, for neither girl looked startled, but Lencia pounced on the bread as it bounced off the deck, then glared up at Pen in fright as if she imagined him snatching it from her. He secured the water bottle instead, to her clear dismay.

"You two can share the bread," he said with an easy smile. "I daresay I've eaten more recently than you." This wouldn't be a charity he could afford for long, given Des's drain on his body, but it served to set the tone. He sat down across from them with the water bottle, freed the cup, popped the cork, and tested a taste. Every bit as murky and vile as he'd posited, ugh. Knees bent up for a shield, he set about some sleight of hand, concealing the trickle into the cup from the air. Seuka watched him, licking dry lips. Her eyes widened in surprise when he handed the first cupful across to her. She guzzled hastily, then hesitated partway down and glanced at Lencia.

"You can drink up. There's more," said Pen, and she promptly did. He alternated handing the cup across to each sister till they stopped reaching, hoping that they wouldn't notice they'd each drunk more than the bottle could hold. Overheating from the exertion, he finished with a cupful for himself and laid the leather skin aside. Maybe he could use its noxious contents later for flushing the latrine corner.

A sound of gnawing, like rats at a wainscoting, filled the hold for a while as the two girls divided the dry bread. While they were working at it, he leaned his head back against the bulkhead, closed his eyes, and took a quick survey of the number of actual rats lurking aboard. Hm, only a few. Destroying vermin was an allowable and efficient sink for Des's chaos when uphill magic, creating order, produced, as always, a greater amount of disorder to dump. Somewhere. Or he could pass out from the fever generated, usually not helpful. Downhill destructive magic was less costly. …Albeit not on a ship in the middle of a trackless sea. Pen opened his eyes to find both girls staring at him again, though no longer in fear. More like fascination.

Seuka pointed to the patches of light falling on the deck, squaring up as the sun climbed toward noon and the sky turned blue. "Sit over there," she commanded him.

"I'm not cold," he said, a trifle confused.

"No, it's…" She waved her hands around her head, and pointed to his. "Do it again."

His brief bafflement was alleviated when Des chuckled, *It's your hair, Pen. Works on females of all ages.*

Nikys likewise, he was reminded, who'd made him grow out his queue to twice its former length, so it wasn't as if he could complain at this attention. He scooted over to a sun patch and sat cross-legged, wryly angling for the best backlight. *It's not magic, curse it.*

Hey, it enchanted us, the first time we ever looked up at you on that dismal roadside in the cantons. Where Ruchia, Des's latest prior possessor, had lain dying.

I thought it was mainly the decided lack of other volunteers, he grumbled. *I was a skinny, spotty, awkward youth.*

Who took our hand and said Yes to us. And to our god.

That had been an unexpected codicil. But the corners of his lips edged up in memory regardless.

His stray smile emboldened the girls, or maybe they were revitalized by the food and water. In this better light, he saw their eyes were a bright coppery brown, suggesting a measure of Roknari blood. They inched closer to him across the boards. "Can I touch it?" said Seuka, already stretching out a small hand.

"Yes, go ahead," Pen sighed, wrapping his arms around his bent-up knees and propping his forehead on them. For his privacy and theirs, equally. Touching quickly turned to finger-combing, as one hand became two and then four, and his hair tie was made away with. Then, inevitably, braiding. And rebraiding, because of course everyone wanted a turn.

Somewhere, there was an important boundary between calming their fears, and keeping enough respect that they would obey his orders in an emergency instantly and without question. He wished he knew where it fell. Though as pacification ploys went, letting them groom him like a pony cost only a little of his dignity.

And it's rather soothing, Des observed.

Hush. But his eyes were slipping closed as his head grew heavier.

He jerked upright before he started snoring, though not before he started drooling. Rubbing at the wet patch on his trouser knee, he said, "That's enough, now," and retreated to his propping bulkhead. His handmaids frowned at him in disappointment, but shuffled back to their own claimed corner.

"When I was being dragged aboard," he began again, "I caught a glimpse of another hold, aft." And he needn't mention that this survey had not been with his eyes. "It had six prisoners in it. Not sailors. Are they other passengers from your ship?"

"Maybe?" said Lencia. "There was only our ship taken, and then yours."

"Are they all right?" asked Seuka, freshly apprehensive.

"Alive, at least. There was an old couple, roughed up. A fellow who seemed to be with them had a broken arm."

Lencia nodded. "He's their son. He tried to defend them, but the pirate hit him with his hammer. It made a horrible sound."

Ah, the war hammer again; it must be a favorite of its wielder. The son, himself middle-aged, was lucky it wasn't his skull broken. In any case, not three people Pen could count on in a fight, or to help sail the ship.

"Another middle-aged man, portly."

"That was the merchant from Adria," said Seuka. "He was nice. We asked him if he'd ever met Papa, but he said no." She vented a glum sigh.

"Another older man, skinny. Dyspeptic...um, grouchy," Pen amended his bookish vocabulary, and they brightened with recognition.

Probably an effect of his worms, murmured Des.

Well, there's some more vermin for you, in a pinch.

An impression of a tongue stuck out in disgust.

"Oh, Pozeni," said Lencia. "The captain told us he was a scribe from Carpagamo, but as the pirates were grabbing him he was crying that he was a divine of the Father, and they'd better watch out."

"So...which was the true tale? Do you know?"

Lencia wrinkled her nose. "I think he was a scribe, and was just trying not to be murdered."

"Fair enough." Pozeni might be fit enough to help sail the ship; probably not a hand for a brawl, if it came to that. "There was one other man. Cut up, feverish, weak from blood loss."

"Yes, he was the other Adriac merchant. Partner to the fat fellow, I think. He tried to fight." Lencia hunched at the brutal memory. "He held them off for a little, but then they got him down and were really mad. I thought they'd killed him."

Pen had been disoriented in the moment, but his own quick surrender was beginning to seem a tad craven to his own eyes.

Not to mine, put in Des. *Even your lumpish army brother-in-law is in favor of living to fight another day.*

And it was a measure of...something, that Pen could actually *wish* for Adelis Arisaydia to hand. Though *What would Adelis do?* was likely not a very useful model for Pen.

In any case, with the exception of the scribe it was plain the occupants of the other hold were mature persons of property, poor prospects as slaves but promising for ransom. No doubt why they were sequestered together. So they didn't need rescuing exactly; they would be invited to rescue themselves, at a cost painful in purse rather than body.

Pen considered whose name he might cry for ransom. Not Duke Jurgo; that would suggest too high a price. General Arisaydia likewise, besides being much too near to Nikys. His best bet was the archdivine of Orbas, who had sent him despite his protests on this ill-fated errand in the first place and thus deserved the debt. Well...all right, the archdivine of Trigonie's request for the loan of Penric to examine a potential candidate for Temple sorcerer had been a legitimate call upon Pen's skills. The dozen administrative chores both archdivines tacked on *As long as you're going to be there, eh?* had been more irksome.

Pen could easily feign to be a favored scribe in his home curia; his name should be enough to alert his superior to his ploy. Maybe? It was a delicate balance, to suggest a ransom high enough to outweigh his profit as a slave, without running up the total as high as it could go. ...Which led him in turn to muse upon just what price *would* make his ransomers choke. What was his value to Orbas?

Less than my value in *Orbas.*

Besides, the Temple was always running on a tight budget.

These Jokonan sisters lay outside all such calculations. Pen wondered if he could attach them to his own bill, *One stray scribe, plus two orphan wards of my Order.* It would be tricky to claim the three of them as a set to whatever middlemen bid on them, when the pirates knew very well they were not.

The day dragged. Twice more scant provisions were dropped down: some hard barley bread, an oddly generous portion of dried apricots that Pen recognized as filched from his own former ship's stores. The edges taken off their appetites, the girls thought to offer back a portion for their new holdmate, which due to the hungry ache in his head Pen now accepted. The leather bottle was raised and lowered refilled. In the dark bilges below, a stray rat quietly died as the price of Pen's pure water shared around.

When the light dwindled, Pen, in place of any too-revealing anecdotes about himself, dredged up some dimly remembered nursery tales from the cantons, figuring that at least they might be new to his Jokonan audience. Translated into Roknari terms on the wing, some of them came out a little oddly, but they seemed to work nonetheless. The girls ended up creeping close to the cadences of his voice and finally falling asleep in a huddle with one head pillowed on each of his not-well-padded thighs. Which left Pen again leaning back propped by the bulkhead, speculating that with Des's aid, rotting out some boards and breaking through the wall was possible, but pointless as long as they were still at sea.

Children, he reflected as he shifted uncomfortably, trying not to dislodge them because surely sleep was a good restorative, attached themselves much too easily to any friendly-seeming adult. Though his persona as a timid scribe did not seem hard to maintain—for all that he walked through the world trailing a discreet cloud of destruction and death as the price of his magic, Pen had never felt less lethal.

Tally: innocent rats, one; murderous slaver pirates, zero. He rolled his shoulders and tried to doze.

THE SUN was climbing toward noon next day when the shifting of the ship betrayed more frequent tacking. Feet thumped overhead, and calls. Pen added a few new terms of ship slang to his vocabulary in two tongues. A rattle of stays and lines, the whooshing thuds of folding canvas, odd groans as ropes and timbers took up slack. *Docking,* murmured Des, relieved. The ship rocked one last time and came to a halt too still to be a mere heaving-to, motionless, blessedly motionless.

Port, five gods be thanked. Maybe.

At length, the grid was heaved up, a rope ladder lowered, and the prisoners were invited to climb out of their noisome hole. Pen made sure the sisters went up safely first, then followed close. He squinted around in the hazy warm air.

Their ship had been tied to a stone-and-piling pier, one of a pair jutting from a rambling shore settlement. Out in the tidy harbor created by a low headland, a few fishing boats were moored, and some larger vessels including, disturbingly, a galley with a long row of oar slots; too broad to be a war vessel, but certainly of Roknari build. The dry green slopes cradling the town rose up to rugged mountains, their spines not high enough to bear snow.

The lay of the light told Pen they were on the eastern side of the sea from Cedonia, therefore on a Carpagamon island, or buffer island. As soon as he discovered the name of the place, he could affix it on the map in his head. But…it gave him some of the same problems of escape as a ship, except that Des couldn't accidentally sink it.

A couple of the crewmen were looking back out to the horizon, hands shading their eyes, scowling. "Where are the bloody fools?" muttered one. "I thought they'd got ahead of us."

They were one ship, Pen realized. Not two in convoy. His coaster appeared to be missing. Separated in the night, and then…? It didn't look as though the pirates knew, either.

The disheveled prisoners from the other hold were being prodded off across the gangplank. No one had bothered to chain them together, and little wonder. An elderly woman limped between two men scarcely steadier on their feet. A lanky, lugu-brious fellow hobbled feverishly, held upright by his very stout companion—the Adriac merchant partners. A last skinny man, presumably the scribe-or-divine the girls had named Pozeni, whined in their wake, protesting to his supremely uninterested guards, one of whom poked at his backside with a short sword and grinned when he yelped.

A pirate dubiously regarded Pen, fit by contrast. "You going to give us any trouble, pretty boy?"

Pen shrugged. "Where's the point? I can't swim back to Orbas."

"True enough." The man smirked, swinging his truncheon to his shoulder and tapping jauntily, then gestured him after the others.

One Corva sister grabbed Pen's hand fore and the other aft as they made their way over the unstable gangplank. He kept hold of them as they veered onto the dock, and they kept hold of him, though Seuka switched her tight grip to his tunic hem. The stout merchant glanced back at them in curiosity. In a few moments the echoing boards underfoot gave way to solid ground at last. Its vague rocking, Pen reassured himself, was an illusion fostered by his time at sea.

Now? murmured Des. *You promised.*

I did, Pen allowed. He'd diverted them both during the fitful night by working out the details, and this needed to be done before they were marched out of range.

Under his guidance, Des ran a line of deep rot through the hull along the starboard side of the keel, bow to stern. On the port side nearest the dock, they unraveled slivers high up on all the stays that held the mainmast in place, leaving a few delicate threads pulled taut. To make sure, Pen ran a thin layer of rot half-through the mast itself, at what he hoped would be the most destructive height. The galley on this ship was rudimentary, a mere sand table under an awning, aft, with coals banked. The supports on one side of the table gave way, spilling sand and hot embers onto the deck. The awning puffed alight.

Truly, nothing increased disorder as efficiently as fire. Pen bit his lip and did not look back.

"Stay close to me if you can," Pen told his small clinging companions. "Let me do the talking. If we do get separated, I'll find you somehow." He hoped this pledge would not turn out to be hollow.

They trudged up the shore to what was obviously, despite this being a pirate haven, a customs shed. Did even pirates not escape taxation? It was a long, low building with a wooden roof, not the more usual stucco and tile, and Pen wondered if it was built of old ship timbers. As the party of prisoners was being chivvied through the door, the first cry of alarm rose from the dock behind.

The man whom Pen took to be the captain, by his age and the way he'd been issuing orders, swiveled around, and he cursed in surprise. "*Now* what...!" He glared at the rising plume of smoke, calling, "Totch, get them recorded. Figure the port fees and the guild charges. You two, come with me," and sprinted back down the slope, followed by two of the three guards.

Which might have made a good opportunity for Pen to try a daring escape, except for his baggage. He grimaced and let himself and his charges be prodded by truncheon-man Totch into the shed, blinking as his eyes adjusted to the reduced light. The air inside was hot and close, with a faint reek of stale urine, old blood, and stressed sweat.

The bare space had only a dirt floor, though a few benches were shoved up against one wall. The fat fellow escorted his injured comrade at once to one of these, helping him to gingerly sit, and the old woman was settled on another by her husband and son. A long table with a few stools occupied the other side of the room, though only one stool was currently in use. Despite his rough garb, the islander who sat there ordering his quills and paper had the air of every customs clerk Penric had ever encountered: middle-aged, ink-stained, underpaid and unimpressed. A couple of big armed men, flanking him, took in the new arrivals with experienced eyes, then drifted back to lean more comfortably against the wall.

"Totch." The clerk waved greeting at the pirate Pen guessed was the first mate. "Is this your whole catch? Falun is in port. He'll be disappointed."

"Aye, I saw his galley." Totch looked over his bedraggled prisoners. "This lot is mostly for ransom. We've two more prize ships coming later, with a fair number of fit men. We were separated from the first a week ago in a storm. The other...should be here. Soon." Pen thought he sounded uneasy in this claim.

"Well, let's get started." The clerk, whose rustic Adriac accent matched his beard, motioned Pen and his hangers-on forward. Pen moved without truncheon-prodding.

The clerk poised his quill. "Name?"

"Penric kin Jurald."

The clerk hesitated; Pen helpfully spelled it out for him. Because in case word did get back to Orbas, he wanted it to be recognized.

"Age?"

"Thirty-two."

The clerk snorted. "Good try, but it won't save your tail if someone wants to buy it, Blue-eyes. What's your real age?"

"Thirty-two," Pen repeated patiently. "Many people misestimate me." *And let's keep it that way.*

The clerk shook his head and wrote down *twenty-two*. Pen didn't bother pursuing the argument.

"Family?"

"None to speak of. My parents died some time ago. Back in the cantons." The latter part of which was perfectly true. The inquiry, of course, was to flush out some gauge of how much ransom might be squeezed out of relatives, so many captives lied. As he was doing, by omission.

"Ah." The clerk pursed his lips in satisfaction at the explanation of Pen's alien name and coloring. "Profession?"

"Scribe. I work for the curia of the archdivine of Orbas, in Vilnoc." True in a sense. "I'll be crying ransom to the curia. Also for my nieces." He let his hands rest on the shoulders of the two girls, who, speaking no Adriac, had hunched closer to him in worry. He hoped this gave his new claim an authentic air. "Keep us together. My ransom will cover all."

"Not up to me. Though I'd think the curia of Orbas could buy a new clerk for a lot less than that."

"I'm very good at my job."

"Howsoever. And those two?" The clerk eyed the girls, who didn't look much like Pen, in jaded suspicion.

"Lencia and Seuka Corva." They both looked up at the sounds of their names. "Daughters of my late half-sister." Yes, as he and the dead prostitute were both children of the white god, perhaps siblings in faith. "She'd been lost to the family for a long time, then word of her fate turned up in Jokona. I've only just found her girls. They don't speak any Adriac."

"Jokonan, are they?" The clerk raised his brows. "You speak Roknari?"

"A little."

The clerk made a pleased note. "Anything else?"

"Well, Wealdean, of course. My mother tongue." Pen realized he might be inadvertently running up his price, but after giving his real birthplace he had to admit to that. Literate translators were much sought-after, slave or free, so the rest of his learning had best stay unmentioned.

"Really? Was her tongue silver? I'd have guessed you were a fancy Lodi lad. Or a Lodi fancy lad. But you must speak and write Cedonian, to work in Orbas."

"Well, yes, that too."

Another note. "Huh. You may be able to save your own tail."

"I plan to." Pen bit back tarter remarks. True or not.

Thankfully, the clerk waved him away before he could tangle himself further, and called up the next prisoners. Pen towed the girls to the freed bench and settled them close.

"Call me Uncle Penric from here on out," he whispered to them in Roknari. "I've claimed your mother was my half-sister, and that I've just found you. It may or may not help keep us together, but it seems the best gamble."

"Would slavers care about that?" said Lencia doubtfully.

Young apparently did not mean ignorant. "No, but they care about ransoms."

"Oh." She pressed her lips together, looking reassured. Seuka stared at him as if he had just performed some amazing magical trick. ...Which he could, but Bastard's tears, not here.

I like these girls, Des remarked cheerily. *Let's keep them.*

At least as far as Vilnoc. Yes, any search for their elusive papa was best performed from the safety of home, at leisure. Preferably by letter—Pen had friends and colleagues in Lodi he might draw upon—because once he stepped ashore he was determined not to leave his and Nikys's neat little house again even if dragged by ox-team. He had ways of dropping an ox-team...

But not an archdivine, Des observed. *Or a duke.*

Or a god. Pen sighed concession. Although if the merchant Getaf was found, he might be persuaded to reimburse the curia for the expenditure on his children's behalf, soothing the comptroller.

The aged family disposed of, the stout Adriac merchant came up next to speak for his friend and beg clean water and medical care, only to be told he had to wait for their next destination, and the less trouble he gave, the sooner they would be taken there. Pen had to wonder what quality of physicians might be found in this backwater. Pirates and fishermen both were prone to dire injuries, though, so perhaps the local devotees of the Mother's Order had practice.

The skinny fellow then proceeded to argue for considerations due to his claimed status as a divine of the Father's Order, which Pen doubted and the clerk did not care about. It only ended when the captain rolled back in, soot-smudged and irritated. Regrettably, it seemed he and his crew had managed to put out the galley fire. That was all right. Pen could wait.

The prisoners were all collected again by the pirates and the armed port-shed guards, to be led on a march up into town. The captain was briefly interrupted by a trio of tough-looking, tattooed townswomen demanding to know where their husbands were, evidently among his crew detailed to bring in the prize ships, to whom he gave temporizing excuses that plainly did not please them. Escaping this hazard, he managed to escort his... *catch*, a revealing term Pen thought, to another large building, this in the more usual whitewashed stucco of the islands. Thick-walled, it was cool and shadowed when they stepped within.

Pen hadn't been sure whether to expect a prison
or an auction block, but this seemed neither. The
front room was spacious and paved with a smooth
cement, a set of stairs at one end leading to the
upper story. *Dormitories, I wager*, murmured Des.
Other passages led off it to who knew what, though
presumably including a kitchen, because some
trestle tables were folded against a wall, and a few
benches were scattered about. Holding place, then.
It seemed underfilled with only Pen's party. Did it
not hold people for long? Although two more ships'
worth of unhappy sailors were yet expected.

Maybe there was some more secure prison for
violent captives. How big was this island? Might
there be wild areas where a runaway could conceal
himself, or other towns or villages with boats? The
sea discouraged Pen, but a trained sailor might view
it as more road than moat.

It appeared the ransom candidates were to be
cared-for, after a rudimentary fashion. First, the
guards herded them all out to a small closed courtyard, where they were permitted a wash and drink
at a wall-spigot that emptied into a trough, draining
from there away to a channel under the wall. Their
several days crowded in a hold no larger than what

Pen had shared with the Corva sisters had broken down any bodily reticence among them, so the men stripped to wash well, sharing around the chunk of coarse soap provided, and the rinse bucket. Pen resignedly bore the covert stares from all alike that he won during this. The chance to scour off the ship-stink was worth it.

The old woman washed by halves, everyone politely ignoring the inadequacy of her old husband's attempt to shield her modesty by interposing his filthy shirt held out as a screen. Pen in turn prevailed upon her to help him with the girls' much-needed ablutions. Pen grimaced to don his dirty clothes again, but he supposed everyone else's changes were on their prior ship as well. Would such personal effects be returned when the ship came in, or just be stolen? He didn't hold out much hope for his own.

While this was going on, an islander midwife with a green sash around her tunic, cursory salute to the Mother's Order, appeared with a kit to attend to the cut-up Adriac merchant, whose name was Aloro, and the old couple's son with the broken forearm. The arm needed to be rebroken and reset, in Pen's view, but instead received some horsing around that left it scarcely improved and the son fainting.

The midwife at least provided him with a sling. She cleaned and bandaged Aloro's sword cuts, several on his arms and a longer gash across his torso. The little ordeal left the man supine and gasping, clutching his fearful friend Arditi's sweating hand till the plump pink flesh bunched white. The wounds were red and ugly with infection, healing barely holding its own.

Don't mix in, muttered Des, uneasy at Pen's restive, reflexive evaluations. *At least till we're sure we can afford it.* Nevertheless, under the guise of assisting the midwife, Pen did manage to slip the injuries a general boost of uphill magic, his reserve from the chaos planted on the ship not yet leaked away.

Back in the main room, an islander man and woman appeared and conscripted the few able-bodied, headed by Pen, to set up the trestles and help carry food from the back kitchen: plain but wholesome fare of flat bread, cheese, olives and sardines in oil, dried figs, and heavily watered wine. Pen was amused when the captives begged 'Learned Pozeni', in his capacity as a divine of the Father, to bless the meal. This he managed to pass-ably do, which incidentally revealed by the return tally-signs that all those present were Quintarian or chose to appear so—apart from the Jokonan girls, who, adrift on the unfamiliar speech, sat mute and motionless. The food was abundant enough that Pen had no need to exert himself to make sure his 'nieces' received their share. So, they were not to be starved into submission.

Upon inquiry, Pen delivered a tale to their table-mates, in urbane Lodi Adriac, about encountering the sought sisters by wildest chance in the pirate hold, surely a blessing of the white god. This dramatic and unlikely fiction was accepted wide-eyed by the old woman, and with narrower skepticism by the rest. Pen wished he could be as sure the mystical assertion was untrue. In return he was gifted with the unlucky travelers' own tales, none remarkably different from what he had already construed.

By the time they cleared the trestles, the relaxation induced by the wash and the meal had Pen swaying on his feet, hoping to be led to those dormitories soon. Both the ease and the hope evaporated abruptly when the pirate captain, whose name Pen had learned was Valbyn, returned, trailed by the port clerk with the sheaf of his pages in hand. Totch with his truncheon tagged along. Two new men, one with an attendant servant, followed them in through the door.

The shorter, sturdier newcomer had dark hair and eyes. The tunic, trousers, and leather shoes he wore might have belonged to any active merchant around this sea, but the rings on his hands were heavy gold, and his sleeveless coat, its embroidered hem swinging at his knees, was richly dyed in a dark red. The younger man who dogged him, carrying a writing box, had similar height and coloration, if more humble dress. They might or might not be related, but they both looked very Darthacan.

Pen's guess was confirmed when the older murmured in that tongue, "Watch out for these islanders. The port officials won't hesitate to collude with the free captains to foist off any rubbish they can't saddle on their Roknari neighbors." The younger man nodded earnestly.

The taller, leaner arrival had skin sun-burnished to a gleaming bronze, possibly enhanced with a touch of oil. His reddish-bronze hair was bound up in a complicated braid around his head, a few artful ringlets allowed to dangle at his temples. A wide-cut sleeveless tunic fell to his ankles, allowing him to sensibly dispense with trousers in this heat. The bleached cloth was caught up at his waist by a belt, studded with colored gleams that might be jewels or glass, supporting a long dagger in a tooled scabbard. Good leather sandals, well broken-in, protected his feet. Like his Darthacan counterpart's, the garb seemed everyday working dress for an established trader, suggesting neither man felt need here to impress anyone.

The two exchanged familiar, measured chin-ducks. "Captain Falun," said the Darthacan. "Good to see you well," receiving in return a slightly dry, "Master Marle. I trust your last business prospered." Both in thickly accented but serviceable trade Adriac, establishing the language of the hour, and the hint that neither was privy to the other's tongue.

"Tolerably, tolerably," said the swarthy Marle. "Yourself?"

"The sea was kind to us, last voyage."

"Always a blessing." The Darthacan, who had to be Quintarian, politely did not suggest from which god.

"Aye," agreed the Quadrene captain, as politely not quibbling.

Signaling business, not theology, was to be the order of the day. Really, Pen was relieved.

The house servants brought out two chairs graced with cushions for the important guests. Customers?

Totch, waving his truncheon more in gesture than threat, had the captives drag over their benches to the near wall and seat themselves, instructing them to line up in a row and keep their mouths shut, and maybe they'd get some good news.

Doubt that, murmured Des.

Mm, thought Pen back. He whispered in Roknari to the intimidated girls, who'd tucked themselves up one on each side of him, "I think one of those men might be here about ransoms. Be quiet and wait, till I find out what's happening."

They both nodded trustingly. Pen concealed his wince at their baseless faith in him.

The Darthacan and the port clerk put their heads together over the entry papers. The assistant opened his writing box and set up to take notes. Captain Falun, Captain Valbyn following, rose and wandered over to the array of captives.

Falun sniffed in disapproval at the old couple. He made their middle-aged son unship his swollen, empurpled arm from the sling and hold it out; pressing long, strong fingers down it, at which the man choked back a cry of pain, he frowned at Valbyn and said in Roknari, "You've damaged this one beyond my use. *That's* never going to heal straight."

Valbyn shrugged. "Marle will take the family whole, then."

"Marle is welcome to them." Falun looked over the somewhat younger pair of Adriac merchants with equal doubt. Or feigned doubt, Pen realized, likely the first moves in some delicate dance around prices. "Same problem with this fellow. Looks feverish to me. Would he even last the trip home to Rathnatta?" He touched a palm to Aloro's forehead; the man jerked back. Pen thought the merchant might be catching a few words of the Roknari, and all of the interplay.

So the dapper Falun was a Rathnattan, specifically; that semi-independent princedom being either the northernmost large island of the Carpagamon chain or the westernmost of the Archipelago, depending on how the map was divided in any given year.

"You could likely sweat the fat off of this one," Valbyn remarked with a nod of his head at the partner Arditi, supporting Aloro as he sagged on the bench.

"Or he would drop at his oar of an apoplexy." Both trader and pirate were haggling in a low dialect of Roknari, with the special endings and honorifics left out, fluid and quick. Pen suspected Falun, at least, could rise to court Roknari at need.

Falun moved on to the skinny Carpagamon. "Really, Valbyn. Can't you do better?"

"He says he's a divine of the Father."

"And you believe him?"

"Doesn't matter to me. If it's true, Marle will scrape his ransom out of the Temple somehow."

Falun stepped along to the next bench. His gaze skipped approvingly over the girls, then rose to Pen and stopped. "Oh." He gave the exclamation a musical lilt, amused and inquiring.

Valbyn suppressed a smirk. "Aye. Claims he's a scribe in the curia of Orbas."

Falun caught up Pen's hands—Pen, pretending to less command of Roknari than he actually possessed, set his teeth and did not resist—and looked them over. "That, I will believe. Daughter's blessings, those are beautiful."

"Goes with the rest of him, wouldn't you agree?"

Falun stared fascinated into Pen's face. "Where are those *eyes* from? I've never seen the like."

"The cantons, he claims. But no family left there. He's relying on the curia for his ransom."

"Seems optimistic." Falun released his hold and stepped back. For once, he did not offer some price-suppressing disparagement. Pen considered coughing in a consumptive manner, but his mouth was too dry.

No matter, said Des. *We can deal with him later. In so many ways.*

Des's prior rider Learned Ruchia had been a sometime-spy, Pen was reminded, if a generation ago in another country. Perhaps that was how Des had learned to listen prick-eared and not interrupt a flow of useful information.

"He claims these Jokonan girls are his nieces," the pirate captain put in.

The Corva sisters, who for a change could understand most of what was being said despite the local accents, both nodded tremulously and gripped Pen's hands as if rescuing them.

"Seems unlikely," said Falun. "Weren't they from two different ships? What does he hope to gain by the tale?"

"Good question, since as far as I know they first met yesterday at dawn, when we slung him into their hold. Future concubines?"

"Or present ones, given some men's tastes. I suppose they'd be grateful." He eyed Pen in new speculation.

Later, Pen schooled himself. *I will take him apart in ways he cannot even* imagine.

Oh come, said Des. *It's a logical speculation from his point of view. Surely you've learned that much about the world by now.*

Bloody-minded demon. Though Des, through some of her less fortunate riders' earlier lives, not only knew the worst of the world but had experienced a nasty share of it. He chose wisdom and let the point rest.

The sisters, insulted on Pen's behalf, were looking mulishly at the Rathnattan trader. Which meant they, too, knew more about the world than was comfortable. He gripped their hands back, silently urging silence.

A call in trade Adriac of "All right," from Marle interrupted this. "I'm ready."

Falun stepped back, and Marle stepped up and joined him, looking unenthusiastically over the captives. Although he blinked when he came to Pen, and pursed his lips in speculation at the sisters.

Falun swept a hand down the row, and said to his colleague, or rival, "You can have that lot, for all of me. I'll take those three." He tapped a finger toward Pen and the sisters.

"Not so fast," said Captain Valbyn. "You'll need to outbid Master Marle."

"What have you calculated for them?" Falun asked, and Marle obligingly extracted the relevant paper from his scribe and showed his arithmetic. Falun frowned. "I'd like a closer look at the blond lad."

Valbyn's lips stretched in a piratical smile. "Very well. Let's take him into a better light."

At truncheon-prod, Pen let himself be marched back out to the little water-court. There, Valbyn shoved him into the full sunlight and made him turn around. Slight gasps from both flesh-merchants made Pen realize the pirate hadn't been easing his captive's discomfiture by setting the examination in private, but rather, was trying to boost his price.

"Make him take off his tunic," said Falun, an order which Valbyn translated. Pen complied. Falun walked around him making muted noises like a man inspecting a horse. A palm to Pen's jaw did not quite result in a perusal of his teeth. Instead, Falun said in Roknari, "He's not *cut*, is he? He's so smooth!"

One of Des's little tricks made shaving as trivial a task as wiping a cloth over his face; maybe he shouldn't have slipped it past during the recent wash-up…

Valbyn, switching back to Falun's tongue, offered, "No, look at his build."

Eunuchs emasculated at a very young age did grow differently, though the one cut man Pen knew as a friend, of sorts, had met his fate well after puberty, and was indistinguishable in outline from any other slim, fit assassin of forty. Except, yes, for his beardlessness.

Falun yanked Pen's trousers down to briefly check, nearly losing his, well, not life, but perhaps permanent use of that arm. The Rathnattan grinned at Pen's angry hiss. Stepping back, he let Pen put himself to rights without further molestation.

"He's been quite docile, so far," Valbyn pointed out.

"Maybe." Falun's bright eyes narrowed at Pen. "If not, it wouldn't be my problem. How many languages do you say he writes?"

"Adriac, Cedonian, whatever benighted tongue they speak beyond the great mountains where he came from, and he even has a start on Roknari."

"Oh?"

"I've seen him whispering to those Jokonan girls. They seem to understand him."

"Quintarian, I suppose."

"Must be."

Falun smirked at Pen and switched back to trade Adriac. "So you think the demon-god will answer your prayers, Sea-eyes?"

Sadly, no. I think the demon-god employs me to answer them for Him. Lazy Bastard.

Des snickered unhelpfully.

Pen managed a shrug in reply to Falun. Some Quintarians with a deep religious calling might risk martyrdom, proclaiming their faith in the teeth of such mockery. Pen thought if his god wanted him martyred, He could bloody do it without Pen's help.

Good, murmured Des. *Keep that view.*

Marle had looked annoyed at being walled off from this dickering by the language barrier, but Pen thought he had followed the play well enough.

They all shuffled back to the main room. The Corva girls looked up anxiously. Pen rejoined them on their bench.

Falun wheeled to study Pen one more time, pursing his lips, then said to Valbyn in trade Adriac, "I'll take him." He named a price in Rathnatta silver ryols that caused the pirate to break into a broad smile, and Marle to frown.

"Master Marle...?" said Valbyn in a leading tone. "Do you care to bid again?"

Marle groused, "The curia of Orbas won't match that for a scribe, no matter how dainty his hands."

Pen cleared his throat. "They might go up a little," he offered. "For the three of us."

"I already calculated for that." Marle eyed the trio on the bench. "And what price are those girls without him? I misdoubt Orbas will ransom *them*. I daresay his curia has never even heard of them. Subtract the scribe, and the girls become near-worthless."

"Not so," said Falun equably. "One can always sell girls somewhere. Though if you don't want them, as a matter of piety I'll take them along and spare them a Quintarian fate."

The two bidders regarded each other, Marle scowling, Falun smiling faintly.

Valbyn gritted his teeth at the impasse, clearly not wishing to displease either customer, then brightened. "A compromise, then. Why don't you each take one. At a slave-girl's price."

Falun's brows flicked up. "That suits me well enough."

"Mm…" said Marle at this lesser consolation. "Not ideal, but it will do."

Valbyn nodded in satisfaction. "Done."

Pen shot to his feet. "No! We have to stay together!" *I promised…*

Totch advanced, truncheon brandished. Valbyn, still in a pleased mood, waved him back. "Now, don't damage Captain Falun's merchandise." While Pen stood fuming, trying to think, he added, "So which of you wants which?"

"The elder," both men said together.

Valbyn vented a long-suffering sigh, and drew a coin from his pocket. He motioned the port clerk over, saying, "Toss it."

The port clerk, who looked like a man who wanted to get home to his dinner, took it without comment, flipped it in the air and caught it, and slapped his other hand down over it.

"Call it," Valbyn said, gesturing to Marle.

After a slight hesitation, Marle said, "Heads."

The port clerk lifted his hand, revealing the reverse of the coin. Marle grimaced.

"Very good, hearty sirs," said Valbyn, retrieving his coin before the port clerk could pocket it. "Shall we settle up?"

Pen stood stiff and fuming. Des murmured uneasily, *Now, don't start a scene here that we can't finish. We aren't leaving harbor on that galley anyway, are we?*

If I have my way, that galley's not leaving this harbor.

Unusual, that his chaos demon should be the one restraining him. It was normally the other way around. More than one battle had been started by mistake, to no one's plan, but yes, if he was declaring a one-sorcerer-war on a pirate haven, it would likely go better with a little advance thought.

"When will you be taking them?" the port clerk asked Falun.

The Rathnattan waved a hand expansively. "They may as well stay here for tonight. I'll wait to sail with a full load, for my profit. What else do you think will make port this week besides Valbyn's prizes?"

"Captain Garnasvik may send back something. He left here a few days before Valbyn."

"Mm. Let's hope he finds fair winds."

Let's not, thought Pen. He sank back on the bench between the sisters.

Lencia tugged at him in worry. "What just happened?"

He didn't want to induce panic and tears, but he daren't lie. He lowered his head and voice. "Nothing is going to happen right away. We'll all be staying here together for tonight, maybe for several days. The Rathnattan slave-trader thinks he's bought me and you. The Darthacan ransom-broker thinks he's bought Seuka. They're both wrong. We're going to do something else."

"What?" said Seuka, looking at him big-eyed.

"It's a secret," he managed after a choked moment. *Even from me, apparently.*

Des, charitably, refrained from laughing at him, but he sensed it was a struggle.

The bargaining conclave broke up. After a final accounting consultation with the port clerk, Falun took his leave, as did Valbyn. Marle and his scribe ushered the folk to be ransomed to the trestle table, settling them down for a more detailed examination of their hopes and resources. The port clerk lingered for this, evidently with an eye to collecting accurate head fees in due course.

Pen and the Jokonan girls were left to their own devices. The armed port guard who'd sat himself on a stool by the door discouraged any premature attempts to exit. Pen, swaying on his feet after several nights of disrupted sleep, not to mention his disrupted life, took the girls upstairs to seek bunks in the dormitories. They discovered two long rooms lined with sailors' hammocks, and also a smaller chamber with actual beds. The slit windows were too narrow even for Pen to turn sideways and slip through, but they overlooked the harbor.

The girls, even more exhausted than he was after their long ordeal, went straight for one straw-stuffed mattress and flopped down together. Pen kept them awake just long enough to divest their sandals. Another bed, motionless and so much more enticing than a bare hold despite the stiff straw-bits poking through the not-very-clean cloth, called to him, but he returned to the window to stare out into the evening light for a few minutes.

Every tactical plan needed to start with an accurate survey of the terrain, or so Adelis had remarked. And a keen evaluation of the physically possible. Some poetic epics extolled heroism in warriors; Adelis the actual soldier put his faith in logistics, Pen had noted. Not that Pen could see much terrain from here, the bulk of the town being in the opposite direction, but by shifting back and forth he was able to take in most of the waterfront. Out on the headland, a ruined fortress was in process of being rebuilt. Pen wasn't sure of the rationale for this, since plainly the stronghold had not held before.

He was about to give up seeking inspiration from the view and also flop down, when Des said,

Ooh, look. Something's finally happening down there. Pen glanced back to the harbor.

At the long dock, Valbyn's ship was starting to list sideways. The slow creep, stretching the mooring lines, converted to a sudden lunge as the first big patch of the hull near the keel gave way. The water pouring into the bilges overstressed the rest of the weakened boards—Pen could hear the muffled cracking propagating even from here. As yet more water roared in, a mooring line pulled its cleat out of the dock, then another did the same. The mainmast snapped abruptly, taking boom, furled sails, and a mess of ropes over the side. The ship rolled and sank till it hit the rocky sand of the harbor bottom with a peculiar grinding noise. Screams and cries wafted up faintly from the shore.

Pen's lips peeled back in something like a grin, only not so nice.

Oh, my, said Des, preening. *Isn't that lovely.*

Yes, there go all Valbyn's profits. And for an added bonus, the wreck would take out a quarter of the port's docking capacity for quite some time to come. Removing that hopeless carcass was going to be a costly undertaking for someone. His glee was muted by the reflection that it would likely be done with slave labor.

This moment of great, admittedly *great*, personal satisfaction did not exactly solve the underlying problems. Sinking every ship in the harbor would leave no way for *Pen* to get off this benighted island.

Still...and Pen wasn't sure if the thought was his or Des's, *who here should next be gifted with an amazing run of bad luck?*

‿◌✦

PEN ROLLED over in the night on his lumpy mattress, reaching muzzily for the warm softness of Nikys. *Ah. No.* He crossed his arms tightly over his chest, wanting her in his embrace but assuredly not wishing her here. Wishing himself there was a separate matter.

His wife didn't know when he'd left Trigonie, nor on what ship. He'd sent no message because he'd expected to be home before it could arrive. So she couldn't yet be worried about him, he told himself, couldn't be in distress, for all that he hoped she missed him in a more general way.

And me, Des put in, diverted by this upwelling of pining.

And you, Pen conceded. After a rocky beginning, Nikys had come to enjoy his resident demon. His mother-in-law even seemed to take Des as a *crony*, which had led to some very odd conversations of a sort Pen was sure few husbands were privy to.

So Nikys was safe in Vilnoc. She sallied forth daily the short distance to Duke Jurgo's household as lady-in-waiting to his daughter, which, since the girl was eight, combined the duties of companion and governess. The palace always sent a sturdy page to escort her home in the evening, there to enjoy the protection of her mother, their few servants, and at present her brother Adelis, back after the Grabyat expedition and also in attendance upon the duke.

...Pen still thought Nikys's garrisoning would be improved by the addition of one Temple sorcerer.

He suspected she thought so, too. Although she bit back any complaints, Nikys had grown tenser at the increasing frequency of Pen's outlying errands, for all that each success had raised his standing in Temple and court.

Well, of course, said Des. *She thinks the reason she never got a child from her first husband was because he was kept so long away from her bed on his military assignments. ...Or at least, she hopes that's the reason.*

Naturally she's afraid of the same thing happening with you.

Right down to the tragic conclusion? Pen certainly meant to spare her a second premature widowhood. As for making the other lapse up to her, pursuing it was the pleasantest task imaginable. ...He trusted his demon's leaking chaos magic wasn't interfering in conception.

It can, but I promise you it's not, Des soothed him. *You haven't been married that long. You merely need a few more months. You should know that, physician.*

Not a physician. I set down that calling.

Hah. Once she is with child, the duke will do her a favor by sending you off to do his bidding. You are going to be just like all those medical students who diagnose themselves with every rare fatal malady they've just learned about. When the time comes, mark you, I am not going to let you terrorize her with all your lurid worries.

He had to smile at the vision. Des was probably just being optimistic in order to buoy him, here in this dark near-prison so far from home, but he granted he was a little heartened.

A rustling and a sigh came from the cot next to his, and a whisper in Roknari, "Are you awake?"

Not meant for Pen's ears, he realized as Lencia mumbled in irritation to her sister, "I am now. Go back to sleep."

"Can't."

"Well, stop wriggling around. And quit kicking me."

"M'not."

"Are too."

A sigh. Then, "I miss Mama. I want to go *home*. I *want* Mama."

"Don't talk about it," chided Lencia, hunching as if hit. "It just makes it worse."

"It wasn't s'pposed to be like this. Why didn't Papa *come?*"

"You saw he never got the letter. He probably doesn't even know about Mama yet."

"Maybe...maybe he came to Raspay after we left. And is following us."

"Well, if he did, he won't find us now. We aren't anywhere we meant to be."

A brooding silence, and a defeated whisper, of, "Yes, I know... I just...don't want it to be so."

A reluctant, conceding hum. "Me, too, Seuka."

After a while, another whisper: "So what are we going to *do*? Mama died, Papa didn't come,

Taspeig left us...that poor sea captain was killed..."
A shudder.

Had that slaughter happened in front of the girls' eyes?

"I don't know. Stop wanting grownups to fix things, maybe. It hasn't worked so far."

"Should we try to run away together?"

"I...maybe. I don't know. That might be worse. If anyone on this island caught us, they'd probably give us back, and then we'd be beaten. Or maybe they'd just make us be slaves in a poorer house."

"At least we'd be with each other."

"Only until one of us was sold. Or both of us."

A voiceless *mm*, like a dog's plaint. "What about Master Penric? He said...uh, I'm not really sure what he said."

A shifting of attention to the nearby cot where Pen lay. He kept his eyes closed and his breathing steady, and refrained from moving.

"I couldn't figure it out either. I suppose he was just blustering, the way fellows do."

"But he seems kind. And smart. He keeps trying to help people."

"I don't think kind is much help against pirates."

"He's pretty enough to be a crow-boy." Seuka considered this. "Or maybe when he was younger, before he became a scribe."

"It looked like that Rathnattan captain who bought him thought so too."

"Does...do you think Master Penric realized? Should we warn him?"

"Don't know. Mama says"—a hiccough—"said, crow-boys are worse-treated than street whores. I'm not so sure about scribes." A hesitation. "Anyway, what could he do if we did? He doesn't look very strong."

"The captain was plenty strong, and the pirates still hacked him to bits." A gulp. No, two gulps, confirming Pen's speculation. "Maybe smart would work better. If it was on our side."

"No one is on our side, Seuka."

A long exhalation. "I s'ppose not."

"Go to *sleep*." Lencia started to turn over, but then, reluctantly, rolled back and hugged her sister close like some bony, awkward, unhappy cloth doll.

The two fell back to sleep before Pen did.

PEN WOKE at dawn and slipped quietly out of their room, careful not to rouse the girls or the old couple and the injured Aloro, who'd taken the other two beds last night while the less crippled were delegated to the dormitory hammocks. Pen drifted down to the kitchen just in time to intercept the house servants arriving to prepare breakfast.

There, for the price of some volunteer labor and charm, he deftly extracted a deal of potentially useful information. The older woman in charge, her lame brother, and a niece proved chatty, interested in the friendly scribe from far away over icy mountains they would likely never see. Pen paid for their tales with a few vivid word-pictures of his birthplace that left him a trifle homesick.

The island, he'd learned yesterday, was Lantihera, an Old Cedonian name hinting at its deeper history; it had once been a possession of the empire, which explained the antique remnant of water system in the back court. More immediately useful, the name had finally placed it on Pen's mental map of the region. The servants' recent personal and local anecdotes were also revealing.

This unprisonlike building was dedicated to ransom candidates, the injured, and the meek. The port—meaning the town, Lanti Harbor or just Lanti for short—was its owner and the little clan's employers. Their work here was seasonal; both pirates and their prey were driven from the sea by the storms that plagued it in winter, the tempest Pen's ship had suffered being an untimely fluke.

Summer was actually, the cook explained to Pen, the quiet time in town, when most of the ships and their crews were out. The rowdies drank and gamed and whored their way through winter, arriving at spring dead broke, if not just plain dead, and ready to raid again. Given the hazards of their trade, Pen was not entirely sure this approach to life was irrational, though the cook spared a nod of admiration for the few notable sailors prudent or successful enough to retire rich, at least by local standards.

A more secure prison for the able-bodied men slated for slavery lay at the other end of the harbor, owned by the guild of fifteen pirate captains who divided control of the port uneasily with the town council. In either location, captives were kept for as short a time as possible before shifting their risks to the flesh-merchants who carried them away. Making Lanti less a slave market than a wholesale warehouse, with people shuffled off in bulk shiploads.

Really, Pen mused, if the Lanti pirates only captured people and goods for their own use, the island would soon be saturated, and the trade would dwindle. It was the middlemen buying the booty and the captives for coin who made the demand bottomless. Pen wasn't sure which half of the traffic he disliked most. Perhaps he didn't have to choose a hierarchy. Lowerarchy?

Slavery was not practiced in the austere cantons, though there remained the question of the continuous export of its men in the mercenary companies, so railed against by the Temple. At least such fellows bartered themselves. During a few historical famines, starving farmers had sold their children to the merchants who came over the mountains from the north for the purpose, events long remembered and resented. Pen wondered what lives the young starvelings had all found in the warmer countries, and if he'd ever met any of their descendants unawares.

All very fascinating, scholar-man, said Des, *but if you want more of the gruesome details, ask Umelan. I don't see need to repeat her experiences in this life. Pray attend to the practical. I can't get off this island without you.*

Yes, yes. Pen smiled as he lifted a tray of bread and olives to carry into the main room, which made the startled cook smile back in quizzical echo.

AFTER SETTLING the girls—who had been thrown into a brief panic by awakening to his absence, and Pen wasn't entirely sure if they'd worried for themselves or for him—overseeing their breakfasts, and working up a little more goodwill in the kitchen, Pen explored the building. An armed guard who seemed more a dozing porter sat outside the front door; even less picket impeded Pen from going out the back way, though he refrained for the moment. The only reading matter he found was an abandoned sheaf of old accounts, which even he was not desperate enough to secure for later. At the end of the upstairs corridor, he discovered a ladder leading to the flat roof, and ascended.

No guards up here; the distances to the nearest other rooftops, too far even for a sailor to jump, made an effective moat of air. The drop straight down to the cobbled streets and flagged courtyard invited leg-breaking. More enticing was an odd tower Pen recognized after a puzzled moment as part of a mast and its crow's nest salvaged from some ship, set up to be a lookout. Yielding to the urge to climb, he lodged himself in its basket fifteen feet above the roof. Not a bad perch—when it was standing still. He imagined it swinging back and forth in high seas; Des, who loathed heights, whimpered at the vision.

He surveyed the town, which the cook had said held some eight thousand souls. Closely crowded stone, stucco, and whitewash in the central sections tailed off to scattered mudbrick, stucco, and thatch on the uninviting hills up behind it. Across the town, diagonally upslope, a dome topped a six-sided stone building not much higher than its neighbors—an old Quintarian temple built in the Cedonian style. A Quadrene temple must also be tucked somewhere, but its architecture was less obvious to Pen's eye.

The snowless mountains would not store water against summer drought. Fishing, not farming, was likely the mainstay of the island people. Piracy was a logical extension of the land's dearth.

He turned back to the sea, glittering in the morning light, deceptively serene. Vilnoc and home lay some two-hundred-fifty miles to the southwest from this spot. It was about four hundred miles south to Lodi and then Trigonie whence, hah, he had started. Three hundred miles north and east, entirely the wrong way, would find Rathnatta-to-be-avoided. Less than two hundred miles straight across, due west, would strike the coast of Cedonia. Currents and cross-winds aside, it was a *country*. Even the rankest amateur navigator could not miss it. Turn left and keep the coast in sight, and eventually one must come to the border of Orbas.

Steal a small boat? That would have been a tempting thought, before Pen's experience of the tempest. Pen had sailed such nimble craft on canton lakes, and even those limpid waters could drown the unwary in storms. Pen and two children in anything he could handle by himself? He might bet his own life on the weather holding fair, but theirs? Were they naïve enough to follow him into that danger?

Bribing a local fisherman to ferry them across would require the man to take them on credit, on Pen's bare word that he would be paid on arrival in Orbas. Finding someone that kindly and credulous on this island seemed improbable. Pen also suspected that while for the pirates stealing from others was all in a day's work, that insouciance did not apply to anyone caught stealing from them. The fisherman's risks could be much sharper than merely that of losing his labor, up to losing his head. Hm.

The Darthacan broker Marle would own, or have passage on, some seaworthy ship heading in the right direction, and have Seuka already with him. Could Pen sneak himself and Lencia aboard, stow away until it was too late to turn around? The news that Pen was sometime-court-sorcerer to the duke of Orbas would catch the man's greed; his sailors might be more inclined to throw Pen overboard. Embarking in any ship that Pen did not himself control bore the same risk.

He'd better find out more about Marle. And Falun. So much depended on which of their flesh-brokers first filled his quota and sailed, and how soon.

Contemplating the sunlit scene, he realized that every possible course of action he might evolve converged to the same point, the absolute need for a boat. *So what I require is the shortest route to one.*

And here came a new one, furling sails and sliding into the harbor. Its draft was shallow enough that it could warp in to the unblocked pier on the farther end of the harbor, where half-a-dozen men came out to catch and loop lines and pull it to a halt. A sturdy gangplank was thrown across to the dock and its deck grew busy, with crew, stevedores, and wharf rats combining to carry off cargo like a line of ants. The line terminated in another customs shed, where Pen was fairly sure harried port clerks took inventory for the town's cut, and perhaps the further divisions among captain's guild, officers, and crew. Some of the nearby buildings must be warehouses for the pirates' ill-gotten cargos. The goods seemed too miscellaneous, the unloading too random and raucous, to be the work of some prudent merchant. Was the ship a pirate's prize? Lencia's and Seuka's first ship, perchance?

Pen's guess was confirmed when a group of men in manacles was marshaled on the deck and marched across the gangplank in chained pairs. Some much more alert-seeming guards than Pen had yet encountered prodded them along at sword's point. Squinting into the salt-hazed distance, Pen counted about thirty heads. They were paraded not to that pier's customs shed, but to a more squat and solid building farther up the shore; they disappeared within. The sturdier slave prison, no doubt, and now Pen knew just where it was.

So, there was a ship. And over there was a crew. All Pen needed to do was bring them back together. Des could go through locks, chains, and manacles like so much paper. And his rescuees would be *grateful* to Penric, a coin he might actually bargain with.

Ooh, said Des. *I fancy that plan.*

Pen wasn't sure if that meant she thought it was the best plan, or just the one that would leave the most chaos in its wake.

No reason it can't be both, she protested.

"*There* you are," called a peeved young voice from below him.

Pen looked down. The Corva sisters stood looking up in vexation.

"You'll get sunburned," reproved Lencia, and "I want to climb, too!" cried Seuka.

Seuka matched actions to words, and Pen's breath hitched when she nearly slipped while stretching for the pegs spaced for a sailor. By the time he'd mustered squeaks of caution, she'd joined him, eeling into the basket. Lencia jittered a moment before swarming up after her. Well, Pen wasn't a heavy man. Their crammed platform probably wouldn't break, though it creaked ominously.

"You can see everything from here!" said Seuka, who likely seldom had an advantage of height.

There was no reason for them to be left as disoriented as he'd been. Pen repeated his little tutorial on regional geography, arm out in a long explanatory sweep. They seemed especially interested in the route to Lodi. Lencia's gloomy glance east, back toward distant Jokona, was blocked by the hills behind.

Lencia repeated her fears for Pen's pale skin in this sun, and Pen let her bid him somewhat imperiously back indoors. He then bethought of a way to divert them from all their anxieties with those otherwise-useless old accounts. Gathering the papers, he led them back to the kitchen where, under the amused eye of the cook, he showed them how to make a serviceable ink with stove soot, water, egg yolk, and a bit of honey, and shape the ends of twigs from the firewood to make writing sticks. At this point, the cook ran them and their mess out, so Pen set up again at a trestle table.

Pen started with a list of useful words in Adriac and Cedonian, and soon had the sisters, heads down and biting their lips charmingly, printing them in two alphabets. They sopped up the new vocabulary with the enviable speed of the young. Seuka drifted from the lesson by drawing a quite recognizable menagerie of a horse, rabbit, dog, and cat, so Pen showed her the words for them as well. He finished by teaching them to recite a short girls' bedtime prayer to the Mother and Daughter, common in both its Adriac and Cedonian versions. This made a useful preamble to easing them back upstairs for the nap in the heat of the late afternoon that was customary in these summer countries for children and adults alike.

He figured he'd be glad of having taken it himself, come midnight.

THE REST of the day passed quietly, with another dinner, and the captives left to putter around the building but not, of course, leave. Under the guise of checking his bandages, Penric managed to slip the feverish Aloro another general boost of uphill magic against infection, leaving the merchant feeling mysteriously eased. "I'm told I have gentle hands," Pen misdirected this attention.

Unlike everyone else in the chamber later that night, the Corva sisters slept the enviably solid sleep of youth. Lencia, Pen was able to wake in the deep dark with a shake to her shoulder and a whispered, "Follow me." Seuka he had to carry out to the hallway, easing the door shut behind them.

"What?" said Seuka drowsily, as he poured her onto her feet.

"Here, hold your sandals and be very quiet. We're leaving."

"I can't even see where I'm stepping," complained Lencia. "How can you?"

The hallway was indeed black, although not to Pen. "I have very good night vision. It's, um, the blue eyes."

"Oh."

"Just take my hands."

They followed him to the stairs in blurry obedience, yawning. Pen had been of two minds about this. Leaving them more-or-less safely here while he scouted the situation risked problems in coming back to collect them, if events went well and fast, not to mention having to get out of the building unobserved twice. Taking them along would expose them to unknown dangers along his route. Neither choice seemed good.

He padded barefoot down the stairs and stopped short, getting his hips bumped by his followers.

There was not one guard as there had been earlier in the day, posted outside the closed front door on a stool, but two, sitting cross-legged on the floor inside the entry. In the light of a candlestick, they were passing the time dicing with each other for, apparently, olive pits, judging by the little arrays before each. They both looked up with unalarmed interest at Pen and the girls.

"Why are you folks stirring?" the elder inquired.

"Cook said she'd leave a bite for my nieces," Pen blurted the first plausible tale that came to mind. He half-raised his hands, each gripped by a sister, to exhibit the supporting nieces. "They've had a hungry time of it."

"Huh!" said the younger guard. "She never leaves *us* anything! How do you get the love?"

The older guard snorted. "Look at him. You need to ask? Women!"

Pen turned toward the kitchen. To his intense dismay, the guards rose and followed them.

The pantry was locked, but fell open quietly to Pen's hand. The older guard set his candlestick down on the scarred kitchen table and went to check the back door. It was firmly bolted, to his evident satisfaction. He returned to thump down on a stool, amiably gesturing the girls to the bench, where they were joined by the younger guard.

Pen rummaged in the pantry, bringing back a bag of figs, a pot of olives, and half of a small wheel of cheese wrapped in cloth. Inviting themselves to the impromptu repast, the guards passed the food around; the younger pulled his wicked belt knife and sliced cheese for his tablemates, kindly handing chunks across to the girls first. The girls both watched Pen big-eyed.

"Oh, look," said Pen hollowly. "Here's the wine." He lifted the jug and plunked it in front of the men. Could he get them drunk enough to pass out?

The younger waved it away. "We don't drink on duty." The elder nodded, though he looked regretful. And possibly a touch resentful of his partner's rectitude. The ban did not seem to apply to the food, each saving their olive pits aside.

The guards then proceeded to *chat*, asking Pen and the girls leading questions about their travels and lives somewhere other than this island. Pen diverted attention from his immediate background by repeating some of his childhood stories about snowy mountains that had fascinated the cook, and which also engrossed the Corva girls. Lencia produced a pared version of their own misadventures, remembering to claim Pen as their mother's long-lost half-brother, so miraculously found. Pen didn't think the bemused guards believed it either.

Evidently, talking to their prisoners in the night watch was a better entertainment for these islanders than dicing for olive pits, and one they'd diverted themselves with before, because they traded back some striking tales from other captives. Rather slyly, the older guard threw in a few descriptions of prior ill-fated escape attempts, variously and sometimes violently thwarted.

Pen was learning a lot about the lives of night-guards in Lanti, but valuable darkness was slipping past outside. He suspected the pair would cheerfully gossip till dawn and the arrival of the kitchen crew, along with all the other hazards of a new day. If Captain Falun decided, tomorrow, that the captured sailors would fill his hold and thus he could sail at once, Pen didn't want to still be here having to navigate twisty new challenges.

Maybe he should have devised some way to lower them all down from the roof despite the height.

Really, said Des, sharing his growing exasperation with this sociable delay. *Those girls are light and young, they would have bounced...*

Pen found himself actually missing his distant eunuch friend, Surakos, and whatever dozen subtle poisons and drugs he would doubtless have successfully concealed about his person. Not to mention that his sale price would probably have topped Pen's own by half. Pen wasn't sure if wishing pirates on Surakos was any more evil than wishing the eunuch on pirates. But the memory of those apothecarial skills did allow him to settle on a course of action at last.

About time, growled Des.

Pen would have preferred to have been touching the guards' heads for this delicate work, but didn't expect they would let him get so near without some violent fending-off. If they continued to sit still, he might manage it safely enough from across the table. He held himself in a moment of unbreathing concentration, called up his full Sight, and ghosted his magic deep into each one's ears, there to gently stroke the interior surfaces of the tiny looping labyrinths in their encasements of bone that seemed to control balance. When he'd been studying medicine back in Martensbridge, injuries and infections in that mysterious organ and their ghastly vertiginous effects had been fascinating problems brought to him for magical healing. It worked just as well in reverse.

Both men's eyes widened, then squinched in nausea. They swayed in their seats, reaching out for support from the table and missing. The aborted motions made it all worse, and they tumbled from their perches onto the kitchen floor. The elder opened his mouth to bellow, but vomited instead. The girls, startled, jumped to their feet.

"Hurry, help me find things to tie them up," Pen diverted them before they could panic.

The younger guard managed to get up as far as his knees before flopping helplessly down again. His cry came out a heartbreaking moan.

"Sorry, sorry," said Pen under his breath, as he hastened around the kitchen looking for strong bindings. A washing line coiled at the bottom of the pantry would do. Hands tied behind backs, feet bound together and hitched to hands, snapping of cords to the right lengths with a touch of chaos. It was a bit redundant—Pen didn't think either man would be walking again for a while—but convincing, which was what he needed. A major value of his magic as a defense lay in its continued secrecy. Once his enemies knew what they were dealing with, they would be much more effectively on guard.

Pen hunkered down by the distressed men's heads. "The poison won't kill you," he told them. "You won't need an antidote. You'll just need to wait out the sick. It will help to lie very still with your eyes closed." He added after an inspired moment, "And don't try to talk or cry out. That would make it worse."

Ungrateful glares, fair enough.

Pen considered, doubtfully, the inadvisability of gagging a vomiting person versus the risks of their shouting for help. Of course, the only people in the building who could hear them were Pen's fellow prisoners still sleeping upstairs. If any woke, and came down, would they be foolish enough to untie the guards? He wanted at least till sunup for a lead-time. Maybe leave a note?

Just go, snapped Des.

Pen nodded and started to shepherd the girls to the back door, the bolt quietly shearing off beneath his concealing hand. At the last moment, he darted back to kneel over the younger guard.

"You really need to get yourself off this dreadful island while you still can," he advised the youth, while helping himself to his sandals and donning them. Pen's long toes stuck out over the soles, but the other guard's boots were even shorter. "Before the life here ruins you. Adria would do. Go to Lodi, and present yourself to my friend Learned Iserne in the curia of the archdivine. Tell her Penric recommended you. She can find you some decent work that doesn't rest on theft, kidnapping, murder and rapine."

A pie-eyed groan was his only reply. Pen patted the young fellow encouragingly on the shoulder and hurried out after the Corva girls.

❧

WARY OF taking a wrong turn in the narrow, crooked streets of Lanti, Pen hugged the harbor shore. The sisters kept a good grip on him. Very few lights relieved the darkness: a mere slice of setting moon, and the lanterns glimmering above the doors of a scattering of inns or brothels that faced the waters. A pair of drunken men making their way home paid them no heed at all. The night air was cool and moist, thick with the dubious smells of the port, fish and salt and tar and dung.

As he led the girls around occasional piles of drying nets and other boat gear, Penric meditated upon rats. Quite by chance, he had lately hit upon a way of brushing light chaos across one spot in the backs of their little rat brains that had dropped them into deep sleep instead of killing them. Sometimes he could repeat the effect. Sometimes the poor creatures just died. Helvia, one of the two prior physician-sorceresses who had possessed Des, had failed to see the value of producing well-slept rats, but Amberein, the other, had been intrigued. She had once treated, with indifferent success, a man who had been brought to her afflicted with sudden, uncontrolled sleeping. That the two effects shared a cause, making the trick extendable to humans, was a plausible guess.

When he reached home again, he must cultivate some Vilnoc knacker to let him experiment on his stock of larger beasts. Because if Pen could work out how to do that to *people* without killing them, it might replace his cruder and more painful tricks, more reliably.

And then practice, because chances were that enemies wouldn't agreeably hold still while he felt their heads, one by one. More likely he'd find himself facing a whole gang of rowdies trying to murder him, and, thus, jumping about erratically. ...The alternative of never leaving his house and Nikys again seemed ever more attractive.

Meanwhile, he supposed he had better go back to his proven standby of roughing up the big sciatic or axillary nerves, inducing pain so excruciating that the victim could not move. And if he misjudged the force and snapped a nerve, at least it would only cripple, not kill.

The whisper—and not from Des—that some men deserved death, he did his best to ignore. Even as a learned divine, it was not his place to judge men's souls. The gods in Their time would do so without fail, and with much fuller knowledge.

Lencia, whose face had been tight since they'd left the ransom house, finally asked, "What did you do to those men?"

"Drugged their olives," Pen offered. He added after a fraught silence, "Not ours, of course." He trusted that questions like *how?* and *when?* would take further reflection that no one would have time for. *You didn't witness magic, no, of course not.*

"Oh."

The bulk of the slave prison loomed at last. Pen led the girls into the nearest side street till he found a niche between two houses, and tucked them into it.

"Lie up here and wait till I come back," he murmured. "I'm not sure how long this is going to take. But if it works, you'll see some activity starting on the pier."

"What if you don't come back?" whispered Seuka.

"If I haven't returned for you by daylight...sneak back to the ransom house. At least they'll feed you there."

Doubtful silence greeted this. He ruffled each of their heads, mute goodwill in lieu of lies, and slipped away into the darkness.

Now it grew tricky, as he'd need to scout and act in the same pass. He began by circling the building, one hand tracing the scabrous stucco, all Des's senses extended. Old ghosts were common in old buildings, sundered souls drifting down into oblivion, but this place seemed to harbor more than its share. He brushed his hand, pointlessly, at one vague shape that pulsed in front of his face like some smoky jellyfish. It had dwindled far past the point of being able to assent to any god; Pen had no means canny or uncanny to affect it. And vice versa, he supposed. *Yes*, agreed Des, *so best attend to what we can do something about.*

On the prison wall above, a few high, iron-barred windows would be susceptible to rusting the rods. At the back, steps led down in shadows to a heavy door with a sturdy lock and a wooden bar, which likely gave onto whatever holding cells lay within. Pen silently unlocked it, unshipped the bar from its clamps, and set it aside, just in case. A higher section of the building, jutting out parallel to the shore, might house administrative offices, unpeopled now. Pen edged around it to the main front door facing the sea and the pier a hundred paces off, where the prize ship creaked sleepily in the lapping of the harbor waves.

Rather more than the thirty sailors Pen had seen enter earlier lay inside; perhaps forty? Residue of an earlier catch? Most dozing, some awake and in pain, none happy. The front doors, also reached by a few steps down, were double, of iron-bound oak so old it might have been iron itself. All susceptible to the three kinds of fire at Pen's command: rot, rust, and flame. But the ornate iron lock was presently unlatched. Pen lifted the handle quietly and slipped inside.

No vestibule; the door opened directly onto a wide front room. To his right was an archway and stairs up to the record-keeping section. Directly ahead lay a locked, barred door to the prison proper. To his left, four men sat around a table under the light of an oil lantern suspended from a roof beam. Passing the dull night playing cards, plainly. Pen blinked his dark-accustomed eyes at the yellow glare.

They twisted around on their stools at his entry, curious but unalarmed when they saw he was alone. The wine carafe seemed mainly there to make their water safer to drink, because they did not look in the least inebriated. One fellow was older, stringy and grizzled. Two were big rowdies. A fourth was a skinny youth. Sergeant, muscle, and runner, Pen pegged them.

Without the girls to safeguard from sudden violence, this time Pen wasn't stopping to chat.

The sergeant had barely laid his cards face-down upon the table and opened his mouth as Pen began to methodically disable the squad. The muscle-men appeared the most alarming, but Pen thought the runner, who could race for reinforcements, was his greatest hazard. One, two, three, four around the table Pen blasted each sciatic nerve with strong chaos, barely short of a severing. He was halfway around again for the work on the opposite legs before the sergeant, rising with a frown, yelped and stumbled to his knees. While the rest attempted to leap up but instead discovered the sabotage coming from their own limbs, Pen made a third pass, stinging the big nerves to their tongues. It wouldn't silence them altogether, but it would certainly muffle their pained noises.

On a ledge above the corner fireplace, unlit in this heat, sat a box of tallow candles. Pen snatched it up. One of the burly guards, now trying to crawl across the floor, made a valiant but futile lunge at Pen's ankles as he skipped past. A couple of key rings strung with iron keys hung from pegs beside the inner door. Pen grabbed them down, hanging the rings on his left arm like clanking bracelets. He boosted the door bar out of its brackets, scowled at the overabundant choice of keys, shrugged, and popped the lock without the mechanical aid.

Stepping down into the deeper darkness beyond, Pen found a central corridor with stone walls, a couple of locked doors on each side. Two chambers on the right, unoccupied. A longer chamber on the left housed the present prisoners. Pen picked a candle out of the box, lit it with a thought, unlocked the nearest door with another—fire and unlocking were among his and Des's oldest magics, and he half-smiled in memory—and nudged it open with his knee. He rocked back at the stench that rolled out.

This is an old Cedonian prison. Doesn't it have drains?

Aye, Des reported after a moment. *There's one down at the end. Meant to be kept rinsed with buckets of seawater. Blocked, unfortunately. I doubt it's been cleaned out since the pirates took over.*

Or since the Cedonians left. Pen took a shallow breath and stepped through.

He raised his smoking candle high, less to see than to illuminate himself for his soon-to-be audience. A few gleams reflected back out of the shadows from widened eyes or bits of metal. Men lay scattered up the length of the chamber on the bare stone floor. They were secured by a miscellany of means, some manacled together at the wrists, some in leg irons, some with hands thrust through locked boards. A brief recoil rippled through them, then a slight, threatening surge forward as they realized the intruder was alone.

To prevent unfortunate misunderstandings, Pen quickly shouted in trade Adriac, "I've come to get you out of here! Your ship is still tied at the pier, and there's only a night watch. You'll be able to retake it together!"

Men stirred, neighbors waking others. Pen bent quickly to the nearest manacled pair and slipped their chains loose. He handed them the keys and the candles. "Start freeing the rest." He stood and shouted again, "Who are the ship's officers?"

A thickset man with a nasty green bruise on his forehead climbed to his feet and staggered forward, holding out his hands trapped in a plank. Before the light redoubled as the first pair shared flame from one candle to another, Pen passed his hand discreetly over the lock and let the man drop the device from his wrists.

"I'm the first mate of the *Autumn's Heart*," he said in a strained voice. "Captain's killed. Who in the Bastard's hell are you?"

"Out of it, I assure you," said, well, maybe Des. Pen cleared his throat and continued, "Was yours the ship taken on its way to Lodi last week, carrying the two young Jokonan girls?"

"Aye..." The man hesitated, squinting with increasing bewilderment at Pen. "Do you know what happened to them?"

"They were...given into my care." Pen didn't venture to say by whom. Or Whom. "I'll explain it all later. Right now, there are four guards in the front room who need to be tied up before they, uh, start moving again. You'll find a supply of things you can use for weapons out there as well—at least, there was a pile of gleanings in the corner that looked promising."

A number of men interned here were injured, mostly roughed up like the mate, but some cut or with broken bones. *Don't get distracted by them now,* growled Des. *You can fool with them later, once we're at sea.*

Right. But Pen added to the chamber, "Let the hale help the halt!"

Movement rumbled through the candle-shot shadows as the men began sorting themselves out. If they were mostly one ship's crew, they must already be used to working together under dangerous conditions, or so Pen hoped. He turned to back to the first mate.

"Once I get you to your vessel, I want you to take me and my nieces—uh, that is, those Jokonan girls—to Vilnoc. There will be some reward for delivering us there. After that, you'll be free to go where you will."

"It's not even my ship. I suppose it belongs to the captain's widow, now. And I've lost all our lading!"

Upset people tended to get tangled in the most useless details, sometimes. "You might be able to make a new start on trade goods in Vilnoc, before returning the ship to the widow. She'll want the

news as soon as may be—better saddened than
endlessly uncertain. Main thing is you have this
one chance to get you and your shipmates off of
Lantihera. Because I've met the Rathnattan here
who is buying galley slaves, and trust me, you don't
want to fall into his hands."

That seemed to focus the man. He nodded grimly.

While this was going on, another sailor had come
up: rangy, skin a sun-darkened bronze, ragged and
stubbled. An equally bronzed and scruffy younger
man followed him. Everyone in here smelled like a
privy, there was no helping that, but they seemed to
have been soaking up the fumes for longer.

"What are they saying?" Rangy asked his partner in Roknari.

"Something about Vilnoc. Or Rathnatta, I'm
not sure."

"We don't want to go to Vilnoc!"

Penric turned and shifted smoothly to low
Roknari. "And who might you be, sir?"

The man grabbed his tunic sleeve. "You can
speak!"

"And listen. How did you come here?"

"I'm just a poor fisherman of Astwyk." Another
island up the Carpagamon chain, Pen dimly recalled.

"They took my boat! It was all I had!" Remembered distress pushed him close to weeping. "Why us? It was just a poor boat! And some fish!"

Pen wondered if he'd be less outraged over richer targets. "The prizes were your persons. Pirates will raid anywhere for those, poor boats or poor villages, as long as they are ill-defended and easy. Like plucking the fruit that hangs lowest on the tree."

"But what's this about Vilnoc?"

"I've come to free you, and we are going to flee to Vilnoc." Assuming his conclusion, but if Pen assumed it firmly enough, he hoped it would stick. "Once we're all protected there, everything else can be sorted out."

"What am I to do in Vilnoc without my boat, without a single coin? We'd just be sold into debt-bondage!"

Debt-bondage was considerably easier to escape than slavery; indeed, most people who fell into it expected it to be temporary. Some were wrong, of course, either death overtaking them before they repurchased or outlived their contracts, or, if they found themselves in a comfortable situation, just settling down reconciled to their reduced status. But Pen could entirely understand the lack of allure.

"If it will reassure you, I can give you my per-sonal guarantee that will not happen." A certainty beyond Pen's own purse; at that point he might have to start calling in favors.

"Who are you to promise that?"

"A man who would make a very bad galley slave."

Which was certainly a believable assertion. The fisherman fell back to confer in his own tongue with the rest of his stolen ship's crew.

Some of the sailors reappeared, dragging in the half-paralyzed and disarmed guards from the front room. One of them took the chance to get in a few retaliatory kicks. Pen's hand landed on his shoulder. "That's not necessary. You can tie them up. Or just lock them in here when we leave."

The man swore and turned on him, brows low-ered, beginning to snap something; but then fell silent, stepping uneasily away.

A sailor pulled one his comrades, clanking, up to the first mate. "None of these keys work!"

Pen sighed and bent to the leg irons. "Let me try. Ah, there." The bolts fell into his hand. The comrade shook the shackles free. All three men gog-gled at him as he rose.

"How did you do that?" asked the sailor.

"There's a trick to it," Pen said vaguely. "It's a puzzle. Like that one with the bent nails." Which had repeatedly defeated him as a child, as he recalled. *Not anymore.* He smirked to himself.

The three said nothing, instead hurrying away to join their fellows who were filing out to marshal their foray in the corridor and the front room. But the first mate frowned back at Pen, and from somewhere in the chamber echoed an unwanted whisper of *Sorcery! He's a sorcerer!*

The mob of them were too noisy to fit Pen's notion of a night raid, but with luck things would go swiftly. The most able-bodied shouldered up to the front ranks, with the injured, mostly helping each other, trailing after. The nervous but determined first mate took the natural lead, or was thrust into it. He had surrendered rather than die before, Pen recalled, but perhaps his unpleasant experiences since had stiffened his backbone.

The Astwyk fisherman meanwhile gathered up his own crew at the far end of the corridor, preparing to escape out the back way, presumably to search for his own beloved boat. Pen didn't think that the surest bet, but provided they didn't impede his own escape he wasn't going to argue with the man. Chaos worked in any direction.

The sailors from the *Autumn's Heart* poured out of the prison and moved off in the dark like a big mumbling caterpillar, more shuffling than charging. But the distance to the pier was short and downslope, and they picked up momentum despite themselves.

Pen hung back till he was sure they'd reached their ship. The wharf guards seemed fire-watch rather than soldiers, and were swiftly overborne by numbers. Pen heard muffled cries and a couple of splashes as bodies hit the water, then the reassuring thump of feet upon a deck, followed by more confidently nautical barked orders.

Pen turned and ran for the side street.

The girls were still where he'd concealed them, thankfully. They hadn't wandered off or even fallen asleep again, but instead waited in a worried huddle. Their breaths hitched as he dashed up, but they didn't recoil or yelp, so presumably they could at least recognize his height and pale hair in the gloom. They rose at his panted, "Come on. Time to go! Run."

They did their best, but Pen's legs were undeniably longer. He tugged them down the street in little leaps, like young deer. "Where are we going, Master Penric?" gasped Seuka.

"I've secured us a ship. It will take us to my home in Vilnoc." If it got away from the dock swiftly enough to outrun pirate reinforcements from shore that would surely be coming along soon, when the noises from the prison and pier were finally noticed.

The sailors already had one jib-sail up, stretching out to catch the gentle land breeze and bestow the first steering-way. A couple of figures scurried along the edge of the pier, casting off lines. "Hurry!" called someone from the thwart, peering landward toward the prison and Pen. "I can see him coming back!" Leaving the lines to trail in the water, the figures pelted from the dock and galloped up the gangplank, which swung and scraped as the ship started moving.

"Hey!" yowled Pen. "Hold! We're here!"

A pair of sailors *looked right at him* and yanked the gangplank inboard. The ship eased away from the pier, the black water below widening. Already it was farther than Pen could jump, and certainly farther than he could toss the sisters, even one at time. *Crow-girls don't fly...* And neither could sorcerers.

"What are you idiots *doing*?" Pen screamed after them.

The first mate hung over the rail, looking unconvincingly apologetic. "I'm sorry! But we cannot be having with a sorcerer aboard. You'd bring us bad luck for sure!"

I'll show you bad luck. I could still sink you from here, you know! Pen, gasping in breathlessness and outrage, barely kept the threat from escaping his tongue. Or, more effectively, from his seething mind.

A couple of seamen stood at the rail beside their leader and made averting holy signs at him.

Pen's return signs were a lot less holy. "You ignorant, ungrateful, selfish sons-of-bitches!" As he stamped along the pier in parallel to their retreat, a torrent of long-unused Wealdean broke from his lips. It was a wonderful language for obscenities, guttural, blunt, and inventively coarse. Wealdean invective had *weight*. It blew his audience back from their rail in brief alarm, but, alas, had no other effect. Even that was lost as the mate cuffed his comrades and sent them to help raise more canvas. At the bow, a spinnaker was haled upward and bellied out, sliding the ship silently away into the night waters.

Pen, halted by the pier's end, bellowed after it, "Bastard's *teeth* I hate sailors!"

HE WAS overheated and dripping with sweat, partly from the run but mostly from using too much magic, too fast. Too carelessly. Too obviously. *Obviously.*

The Corva girls, Pen discovered as he wheeled, were hunched together staring at him in deep dismay.

He hardly needed his dark-sight, raking the shoreline, to spot more trouble on its way. The wavering torches were clue enough. He switched to Roknari. "We have to get off this pier and hide. If they don't see us, chances are they'll think we escaped on that ship, which will buy us time. There's no going back to the ransom house now."

Because if the sisters took refuge there, they would presumably be separated according to the original sales agreement, one sent north, one south, despite the missing Penric. How angry, and at whom, was Falun going to be to discover he'd been sold a false scribe? It occurred to Pen, belatedly, that the revelation of his true calling might protect him from being carried off on Falun's ship. What would happen instead was extremely unclear.

"Are you really an evil sorcerer?" whispered Seuka. And when had she learned to understand that word in Adriac?

Pen rubbed his face in exasperation. "I am really a *Temple* sorcerer. Very tame. Learned Penric. Divine of the white god, graduate almost with honors of the great seminary at Rosehall which…you've never heard of, right, never mind. If I were an *evil* sorcerer, I would have sunk those thankless Adriac scum-suckers." Or set the ship on fire. That would have been gratifying. And spectacular. A lesson all around worth half-a-dozen sermons. He'd missed a teaching opportunity.

Now, now, I was quite impressed with your restraint, murmured Des. *Perhaps the white god knew what he was doing after all when he gifted me to you.*

I'm glad someone did, Pen fumed.

"Weren't you casting a spell?" said Lencia.

"It *sounded* like magic words…" said Seuka warily.

Better awkward questions than screaming and running, Pen supposed.

"Only cursing in the ordinary way. In Wealdean. Which is an entirely unmagical language, I assure you. Magic doesn't work like that." Grabbing and dragging them wasn't a good choice just now. Pen waved his hands attempting to herd them instead. "Move, move! The pirates are coming." Beleaguered, he added, "I'll explain all about it once we get somewhere safe." *Temporarily safe.*

It appeared they were marginally more afraid of pirates than of sorcerers, or else wildly curious about him, because they turned to stumble off the pier at last. Pen led right, angling away from the shore. As they plunged into the deeper shadows of the narrow streets, the sisters reluctantly took Pen's hands again. It wasn't as if they had anyone else's hands to take.

Where are you guiding us now? inquired Des.

To that Quintarian temple we saw from the crow's nest. It should be somewhere on this side of town, uphill. Help me navigate.

To be sure, but if you are thinking of taking refuge there, you may be optimistic. For all we know it's been reconsecrated as Quadrene. Or turned into a warehouse.

If the latter, so much the better. I just need a place to think. Again. Two good plans, ransom and mass escape, had turned to wet paper in his hands because other people wouldn't be sensible. Maybe he needed a plan that didn't rely on other people. Or being sensible.

They only had to backtrack from blind alleys twice before they came out on the narrow square fronting the temple. It featured a fountain serving the nearby streets, running feebly. Dawn nipped their heels, the sky above the eastern hills growing steely, as Pen led the way under the temple's front portico. A lantern hook dangled, but no lantern hung on it. Brought in at night for fear of theft? Pen snorted at the irony and tested the lock on the double doors. It did not give way easily, though more due to corrosion than complexity. No people inside right now. He slid through, motioned the girls after him, and eased the door shut.

Not a warehouse, at least. Pen counted five altars, one against each wall, and breathed relief, laced with stale incense, for Des's other pessimism disproved. A modest clerestory between the shallow dome and the walls, an oculus above, and narrow arched windows over each altar would shed light— in the daytime. The fire on the holy plinth in the center had burned to cold ash, overdue for raking and relighting. Someone was slipshod, or else firewood was excessively dear, here. Or both.

"Is this a safe place?" said Lencia, her voice tinged with doubt.

"For the next hour or so, probably. Until they open up for the day."

Musty prayer rugs and cushions were stacked beside each altar, ready for use by supplicants. Pen pulled some from the Bastard's niche and piled them three high on the stone floor before it, placing the cushions for pillows. "Here. You can at least lie down and rest for a bit while I look around."

"Is that all right with the god?" said Seuka. "I've never been in a *Quintarian* temple before…"

"It's not so very different," said Pen, then realized he'd never been in a Quadrene temple, either. *Four-fifths true*, Des assured him. "As for the white god, I have something of an arrangement with Him." A sometimes-dubious arrangement, but certainly intimate enough to share bedding. Whether this temple's keepers would agree was yet to be explored.

The girls settled, but did not lie down, frowning at him though the shadows. Pen didn't think they could make out much more than a smudge of his face and gleam of eyes and hair. Well, and his smell, drying sweat and filthy clothes, but everyone shared that. Maybe they should have taken yesterday afternoon for laundry instead of language lessons.

"So, um," began Lencia. "How long have you been a sorcerer?" A very grownup conversation opener, apart from the slight quaver in her voice. A ten-year-old terrified orphan, trying to be the grownup, right. Pen bit his lip and simplified.

"Since age nineteen. I was riding down the road near my home and chanced upon a traveling Temple sorceress, elderly, who had suffered heart failure. I stopped to help, but she was dying. A creature of spirit, like a demon—or a human soul, for that matter—cannot exist in the world of matter without a body of matter to support it. Finding me agreeable, the demon jumped to me." *And my future was wholly changed.*

Improved, I trust, murmured Des.

Don't fish for praise. But Pen had to suppress a smile.

"You were *possessed* by a *demon?*" whispered Seuka in shock.

"Are you still?" added Lencia, a little swifter at the implications. She edged back on her rug, though not as far as the hard stone.

"No, I took possession of the demon. And consequently its magic. That made me a sorcerer. Who's in charge is a very important distinction. We call it the demon ascending when it's the other way around. And then actual Temple sorcerers and saints have to go iron things out." This was not the time or place to go into those messy details, Pen sensed. "After that I trained to be a divine. It's usually the reverse order, a person trains before the Temple gifts them a demon, but our case was an emergency. She's like a voice in my head." *Who argues with me.* Best leave out the twelve-fold complications of that, too.

"Your demon's a *girl?*" gasped Seuka.

"Mm, in a sense. Her name is Desdemona."

Given the tight lips and wide eyes of his audience, this wasn't helping.

"She gets along very well with my wife," Pen offered in his demon's support. "Which is good, because it can be a bit like being married to two different people living in the same body."

Lencia's mouth fell open. "You're *married?*" By her tone, his possessing a wife was even more startling than his possessing a demon. Well, in this case perhaps he was the one possessed, and delighted to be so. *Keep simplifying.*

"Yes, we live in a little house in Orbas, together with her mother. Some men don't get along with their mothers-in-law, but we're quite taken with each other. It's nice there." Or was, before he was sent off on a fool's errand and *captured by pirates.* And the sooner he remedied that, the better. He wasn't sure if the girls were actually finding this spate of domestic detail comforting. "I really do serve the archdivine of Orbas. Who lends me to Duke Jurgo, if there's a problem he wishes to set me to. I can get on with my own studies in between, so that works out. But under it all, always, I work for the white god." *Will or nil.* "Who is the protector of orphans, in Quintarian theology." He waited a few moments for this broad hint to sink in.

The wariness did not ease. Pen soldiered on. "So, I've told you all about me. Tell me something more about your mother." *Jedula Corva,* they had let slip her name during those long hours in the pirate-ship hold. "Was she a secret Quintarian? Which god signed her at her funeral?" Both the girls' parents had prayed for their safety, he had no doubt, but only one had certainly met a god face-to-face. Once.

A jerk, a flinch; an increase, not a decrease, in tension. Lencia swallowed and said, "The demon god isn't allowed to sign at a Quadrene funeral."

"A fifth of the time, that ought to be a problem. How do the Quadrene divines in Jokona prevent the white god's sign from being received?"

"He doesn't have a fish," said Seuka, with an everybody-knows-that shrug.

Aye, said Des cheerily. *Fiddle the actions of the funeral animals, which granted is easier when it's four fish swimming in a tub and the divine calling interpretations. Or, if they can't do that, feign the soul is sundered. They'll only admit the truth if they are very annoyed with the deceased or their family.*

Which Pen had heard of, yes. *Quadrenes must believe they are up to their knees in ghosts.* He wondered how offended he should bother to be on behalf of the Bastard, given that the god and His assenting souls danced away together quite beyond the reach of any human chicanery. It was only the living bereaved who were shortchanged. ...Or relieved, he supposed.

Coin toss, agreed Des. *Even in Quintarian lands.*

But Pen was after more particular information. *Let them tell what they know.*

"She was signed by the fish of the Mother of Summer," Lencia said at last. "The divine said. On account of her being a mother. But..." She trailed off, guarded.

Seuka, less discreet, announced sturdily, "But that wasn't what she told *us*."

Pen leaned his back against the Bastard's altar table, the gritty flagstones cool under his haunches, and pretended to be relaxed. "Oh...? And what did she tell you, and when?"

The gloom of the chamber was receding as the sky paled over the dome's oculus. The two girls looked at each other as if for permission or encouragement, then Lencia said, "She was very feverish."

Memories were slippery stuff, but some were stickier than others. Pen still remembered unwanted vivid details from his own father's feverish deathbed, and that was getting on for two decades ago. So he didn't think it pointless to ask, "What precisely did she say?"

Seuka frowned. "She had Taspeig bring us in. She couldn't breathe very well."

The scene plainly rising behind her pinching eyes, Lencia continues, "She said, 'You're going to be all right. I've been bargaining with my body all my life, why not my soul? I've given you into his hands in exchange.' And then she choked for a while, and Taspeig held her up to drink, and she said, 'Best coin I've ever been offered, from a more reliable client.' And then she choked some more, and waved her hand, and Taspeig sent us out."

"We didn't know she was going to die that night," said Seuka, gulping a little. "Afterward, I thought she meant one of her regular fellows was going to adopt us. But that didn't happen."

"She didn't say a name," said Lencia. "Taspeig said she didn't to her, either."

It would be strange even for a feverish woman to entrust an oral will to two children who couldn't possibly effect it. A servant was a barely better witness. The crow-woman appeared to have managed a decent independent life for herself and her children, by the standards of her trade; not the glamor and riches of a high-class courtesan like Mira of Lodi, but not the degradation of the streets, nor even the protection of a brothel at the cost of autonomy. But their own little house had been rented, and there could not have been much else left to them or the girls would have been snapped up by someone in Jokona. And probably stripped of their bequests in short order.

What a bold courtesan! murmured Des, sounding impressed. *Even Mira never bargained with a god!*

If there's a coin that moves the gods, I'd like to know it.

You already do. Her soul, of course.

You think she threatened to sunder herself? Pen's breath drew sharply in. The words hadn't sounded like a woman in despair, but any soul might deny the gods that much. And some women were known to make fantastically heroic self-sacrifices for their children.

Not at all. I think there was another goddess standing near her bedside, bidding for her. For the Bastard to slip one of his best-beloved out from under the nose of the Mother of Summer at such an auction? He might promise much.

The gods, Pen was reminded yet again, didn't value people by the same measures people did. The great-souled and the great saints weren't found only among great men, or even very often so. Of course, the humble were more numerous to start with. Would it be possible to do some sort of holy head-count, and determine if blessedness was evenly distributed? Maybe not; the high were much better recorded than the low. Maybe no merely human eyes were fit to see why the god had so valued this daughter of His.

But in trying to guess why these two sisters seemed so prized that the god of mischance would dump one of his own sorcerers into their hold, maybe Pen had been looking in the wrong direction. *Not destiny, but heritage.*

An appalled grin threatened to stretch his mouth. *What, so the white god has drunk up His chosen soul like a merrymaker at a tavern, and rolled out leaving* me *to pay His bill?*

It was a rude way to think about the gods, but the Bastard could be a very rude god. And, truly, the gods could do nothing in the world of matter except through beings of matter. A doctrinal point Pen had constantly to explain to people trying to pray for good weather or no earthquakes, who never listened, he'd finally decided, because they didn't want it to be so. The gods did not control the weather. Or the world. Or souls.

But death, oh, they own *that.*

Pen made the five-fold tally of the gods, touching forehead, mouth, navel, groin, and hand spread over his heart, then raised his fist to tap the back of his thumb twice against his lips—the thumb and the tongue being both the special symbols of the white god, for good or ill depending on one's beliefs. "Your Jokonan divine lied," he told the girls. "I think that Jedula of Raspay went into the hands of her white god as heart-high as the betrothed at a wedding feast. And found great comfort there. The rest," he sighed, "is up to us."

Pen wasn't sure if the girls took this in as faith or just as proof he was benignly mad.

But, "Oh," said Lencia, and Seuka swallowed, looking as near to tears as he'd yet seen her. Was it from their mother that they'd learned not to weep in the face of fear?

Fear is easy. Joy is hard, said Des.

Mm.

Pen levered himself to his feet. His overstrained body had stiffened while he sat, but this listening had been worth it. "I need to find a better place to hide you before people begin stirring. I'll be back shortly."

A DOOR in the wall next to the Bastard's altar led to the back premises. Pen slipped through and found himself under a short colonnade. To the left, a high gate led out. Ahead lay not so much a temple complex as a temple simplex, a typical rectangular stone building around a central court which had its own small fountain, presently dry. Stairs and a wooden gallery served a course of upper rooms.

Residents? Pen asked Des.

Only three right now, upstairs sleeping.

There should have been rather more, even for a small neighborhood temple. Pen took a quick circuit under the gallery. A room for the divine to change his robes, an office and library, a kitchen along the back, refectory, storerooms, a lecture room converted to a lumber room...that last seemed the best bet for a temporary den, or else an unused room upstairs.

Pen returned to the colonnade and checked beyond the gate. A stable for the sacred animals was built against the outer wall, with a low, slanting roof. The old timbers were sturdy and elaborately carved. New repairs were crude. The long shed seemed currently underpopulated, with a pen of chickens, a couple of nanny goats, and a dozing donkey flopped in its straw. The menagerie seemed less hallowed than practical, not that it couldn't be both.

Pen returned to the temple hall. His breath caught and his steps quickened as he heard a voice grumbling, "Who left this door unlocked? ...Hey! You street rats can't sleep in here!"

Dawn light leaked through the oculus, the arched windows, and, now, the front door, shoved wide. A fellow—townsman or peasant, hard to tell by his plain garb—stood beside the fire plinth with his hands on his hips. He bore a rack on his back holding a bundle of trimmed branches, which he doffed and swung down to the floor. He opened his mouth to shout again at the trespassers, but his jaw hung slack as Penric came up beside the girls, who were pushing themselves up from their rugs, sleepiness warring with fright.

The wood-carrier stepped back, his hand going to the knife at his belt. Pen could see the calculation on his face as he attempted to average the threat: tall strange man, danger; small children, not. And Pen bore no visible weapons; better. The firmness returned to his spine.

"You can't sleep in here. Off with you quick, now, and I'll say no more." His strong island Adriac accent went with his sawed-off, sturdy island build.

Pen suppressed his frustrated curses and let the cultured tones of Lodi infuse his own voice. "But I have quite a lot to say. To begin with, who are you?" Temple servant, obviously, to be bringing in the morning's firewood for the plinth. Or the kitchen, as might be.

The man's face pinched in suspicion. "Brother Godino. I run this place, as much as it gets run."

"I need to speak with the divine."

"You already are. As much as there is one."

Pen's brows rose. "This temple has no trained divine? Or acolyte?"

"It did. Once." Godino scowled at him, and as an afterthought extended the glare to the girls.

Pen hesitated. Would this work? "I am Learned Penric of Orbas. I claim sanctuary in this temple, by the gods' sacred aspects and the rights of my vows, for myself and my wards."

Godino clutched his hair and vented a horrible huff of a laugh. "Oh, gods. You're escaped slaves, aren't you."

"Escaped I'll grant you. Slaves, not yet."

"And so they all say. D'you think you're the first to try this? There is no sanctuary to be had here from the Guild. They go where they want and do what they want, and when they come to drag you back out, I *might* be lucky to only get a beating for having seen you and not cried 'ware at once."

"I don't think it would go like that." *At first.* Though if his enemies brought enough men, even a sorcerer would be overwhelmed, so that was a situation to avoid; he could agree with Godino there. "But the pirates believe we escaped on a ship last night. If you hid us, there would be no reason for them to come searching. We could evade notice for quite a long time."

"And then what?"

"And then you could send a message for help by Temple courier, and someone would arrive to take us off your hands."

"Aye, whisking you off on a magic bird, no doubt, and leaving me here to take the brunt of the Guild's anger? Setting aside there's no courier here either. If you're that much of a somebody, you can ransom yourself and leave me out of it."

"I"—Pen scratched his head—"may have peeved the pirates, a bit. I'd rather not count on ransom."

Godino stepped back and pointed at the door, his hand shaking. "*Out!*"

Penric cleared his throat and said diffidently, "I, ah, hadn't been going to mention this, but I also happen to be the court sorcerer of the duke of Orbas." Well, on occasion, but this did seem to be a moment to raise his repute. "I really do think you will find it in your best interests to help us."

Godino choked on a laugh. "Good one, Lodi fancy-boy. You're no more a sorcerer than you are a divine. *Out!*"

Des...?

Oh yes.

Pen held out his arm dramatically aimed at the plinth and snapped his fingers.

A gout of flame whooshed up seven feet in the air, with a brief roar like an angry lioness.

Godino leaped back uttering an oath. The girls scrambled onto the same mat and clutched each other in voiceless alarm, laced with bug-eyed fascination. The stagecraft was unnecessary for lighting the fire, except perhaps under Godino. With very little charcoal in the ashes to feed upon, the flames died down quickly, but Penric thought the point had been made.

"I am a Temple scholar and learned divine," Penric intoned, "graduate of great Rosehall and chosen of the white god, and I am here to relight your holy fire. One way or another. By sorcery if necessary." He gathered himself and a memory of one of the more daunting sermons of his experience, and thundered, *"Do you understand?"*

Penric thought Godino understood he'd been trapped between murderous pirates and a wrathful sorcerer, and the pirates might be more numerous but the sorcerer was *right here.*

"Yes," he squeaked, wide-eyed. His glance shifted toward the door.

"And don't try to flee, either," said Penric. "You can't outrun magic." Well, he could, but Pen felt no obligation to explain how. He strolled forward, feeling something between gratified and mildly

ill. Bullying a Temple servant was so much easier
than bullying pirates. For real villains, mere threats
would not suffice, and then things would grow ugly.
Uglier. But he needed to get this man under control, and quickly, or their sole advantage left from
last night's debacle would be lost.

"Hide us now," said Pen persuasively. "You can
always betray us later. ...Or try to."

The edged smirk he sent with this made Godino
flinch. Pen could see the moment the man gave in
by the shrinking of his shoulders. Godino set his
teeth on something that might have been a prayer
or the reverse, and muttered, "Come this way, then.
Keep quiet. The fewer who know of you here the
better."

The girls had been following this only with their
gazes, shifting anxiously from one terse speaker to
the other. Pen urged them to their feet, repeating the order for quiet in Roknari. Meek mice, he
thought, had not been that lively pair's role at home
before their world had caved in, but they had surely
learned it in the past weeks. Lencia grasping Seuka's
hand, they practically tiptoed in Godino's wake,
wary of yet another untrusted stranger in an unre-
lenting parade.

He led them up the gallery stairs and into what looked to be a disused temple guest room, containing two narrow beds, a washstand, an old chest, and tattered rugs. Some moth-eaten hangings were piled in one corner; a decent-enough commode chair with chamber pot was tucked in another. The thinness of the dust suggested months rather than years between cleanings, but it still made Lencia sneeze.

Pen stepped around their guide to examine the high window secured with a carved wooden lattice. Wide enough for Pen and, if necessary, his charges to slip through, and overlooking the stable roof; an acceptable escape route, good. Any attempt to lock them in would also be futile, not that Pen was going to point this out. Though Pen suspected Godino would actually be glad for them to bolt, as promptly as possible.

Godino closed the door softly before he spoke again. "You can stay here for the moment. People will be about soon, so don't make noise. We have a funeral this morning."

"Oh? Who for?" Pen hoped he hadn't left any corpses in his wake last night attributable to his magic.

If there were, we'd have known it, said Des grimly.

True.

"Grandmother from down the street. There'll be a lot of relatives."

Life, and death, Pen was reminded, went on quite aside from pirates. "Do you conduct it?"

"Aye... I picked up how by watching Learned Bocali before me. The gods don't seem to mind." He regarded his visitor with new suspicion, as if he expected some sacramental critique.

Given that Pen looked and smelled neither learned nor divine just now, Pen supposed it must be the convincing Lodi accent. He just said, "I expect not." And added, "The children should have clean water first, though. Food when you can. Then we need to talk."

"Huh." With this dubious monosyllable, the temple man retreated.

He returned in a few minutes to tap almost inaudibly on the chamber door, wordlessly handing in a water jug. Pen murmured thanks, and turned back to take stock of his revised set of problems. Again.

"Are we safe?" asked Seuka.

Pen rubbed his tired face and answered honestly, "Not till we reach Vilnoc. But I don't think we can do better right now."

The girls had only had a couple of hours of rest last night, and Penric none. When he'd watered them, had them wash up a bit, and tucked them into one cot, a yawning young head at each end and bare feet tangling, they quickly recaptured the sleep they had almost managed in the temple hall. Pen, lying down tensely on the other cot, envied them for that.

Could they do better for a hiding place? On his own, Pen could probably have gone to ground in his choice of a dozen different holes, feigning any of a dozen different roles. As it was…maybe not. By training and habit, temples felt like refuge to Pen, though it was true that the gods were no more present at Their altars than they were everywhere else. *Nor less, I suppose.* Temples were for the convenience, and perhaps concentration of mind, of their human builders. Pen by his rank also usually had the silent backing of a formal Temple hierarchy that appeared to be lacking here; Godino seemed a very slim reed to lean upon.

Despite his doubts, his exhausted body apparently decided this place was safe enough, because Pen couldn't tell when he slipped into sleep.

HE CAME awake abruptly when the door squeaked open, shooting up in his cot with a gasp, gathering Des the way some men might reach for a sword. *Right here, Pen.* But it was only Godino, returning with a basket on his arm. Alone, not shoved forward by some gang of murderous pirate rowdies. The room was dim, but the angle of the dusty sunbeams and bright patterns of light splashing on the rugs from the latticed window suggested it was a little past noon.

"Food," said Godino gruffly, setting down the basket on the washstand. He stood back and stared at Pen as if afraid he might set something on fire again.

"Thank you," said Pen, sitting up on the edge of his bed as his heartbeat slowed. He investigated the contents, finding flat bread rounds, olives forever, cheese, some of those dried fish planks that people around here thought were food, and, blessedly, boiled eggs. The basket also harbored a jug of red wine and four clay beakers; the number was explained when Godino pulled up two stools, sat on one, and conscripted the other for a table. Maybe Pen wasn't the only man who wanted to talk?

Pen's shaky reserves, drained by last night's exertions, voted for eating first. He peeled an egg and popped it into his mouth while Godino watered wine for two. The temple man cast a glance at the still-sleeping girls and lowered his voice to a murmur.

"There was gossip at the services about the escape of a ship named the *Autumn's Hand* last night. Some say the crew was freed by a poisoner. Some said it was a magician, cloaking himself in smoke and light, casting terrible spells. Some think it wasn't either, just the guards making excuses for themselves for being overpowered. Which given they're bound to be punished, seemed pretty likely." Godino regarded him steadily, and not for the first time Pen wished Des's skills extended to mind-reading.

"And which do you think?" mumbled Pen around a mouthful of bread and cheese.

"If you hadn't shown up here, I'd have guessed the last, too."

Pen cleared his voice with a swallow of watered wine. "Any suggestion the pirates are still looking for this magical smoky poisoner here on Lantihera?"

"Not so far," Godino admitted grudgingly.

"How reliable is your gossip?"

"Some in the neighborhood work for the Guild, one way or another. Lots of folks, really, all over Lanti Harbor, since the rovers are the ones with the money to hire. Not just as crew or rowdies, either, or taverners, but decent work like boat carpentry or ship chandlers."

"How did the pirates come to control this island?"

Godino shrugged. "There were always a few put in here, to offload their goods or captives, and resupply. Smugglers as well. When Carpagamo kept a garrison here, they regulated them and collected the port fees. Rathnatta the same, whenever one of the princes held us.

"Then about ten, fifteen years ago Carpagamo had one of its wars with Adria, and withdrew their men for work closer to home. Usually that's a signal for Rathnatta to move in, but they were having their own war just then among three brother-princes for succession to their dead father's seat. And that's when the pirates ganged together and set up their own conclave."

"Did no one on the island resist this?"

"Eh. Better the rovers should work in one crew than fight each other all over town and make a wreck of the place. And with no taxes being paid to either Carpagamo or Rathnatta, money was less tight, profits rose, and more pirates came. Before we knew it, the town belonged to them, either by coin or by the sword." Godino sighed. "At some point I expect either Carpagamo or Rathnatta will remember us, and muscle back in. No one's much looking forward to that, either."

"Hm...?"

"When Carpagamo's here, the Quadrenes suffer. When it's Rathnatta, it's us Quintarians. At least the Guild makes sure any preying on the local girls gets paid-for." Godino frowned at the sleeping sisters. "And the pirates leave both temples alone, pretty much. Unless someone does something really stupid, like trying to hide runaway captives." His mouth tightened.

"You said this temple once had a divine. Was he under the rule of the archdivine of Carpagamo? Did he leave with the garrison?"

"He wouldn't. Later, I wish't he had." Godino stared at his sandals. "I started here as a boy groom, looking after the holy animals. We had some really nice ones, then. I rose to head groom pretty quickly. After the Guild moved in, some escaped captives came one night to beg sanctuary in the temple just like you did. Learned Bocali stood right there in the portico and told the Guildmen that if they wanted the suppliants, they'd have to go through him.

"So they did. It was a short fight, since he had no weapon but a brass candlestick. Our acolyte was struck down trying to defend the altar treasures, which the rowdies said they were taking for a fine."

The current altar gear, candle- and incense-holders and oil lamps, had all been cheap pottery, Pen realized when he thought back.

"Theirs were the first two funerals I ever conducted by myself, next day, for lack of anyone else. And then I just…kept on. Since people didn't stop being born or needing ease or dying. Carpagamo Temple never came back for us, never sent anyone else out"— he looked briefly as though he wanted to spit—"and Rathnatta, well, I sure don't wish for them."

Pen massaged the back of his neck, which was tight and aching. "I see." Godino might be an unlettered man, Pen thought, but he was neither stupid nor unobservant. Nor unfaithful. Just…vastly overmatched. It sounded as though he'd been eye-witness to the bloody murders, too, which clearly had left a deep impression.

Pen's glance at the other cot discovered both girls with their eyes open, listening worriedly to the baffling Adriac. He told them in Roknari, "Brother Godino has brought us some food. It's after noon, so time to get up. Try not to thump too much."

There followed a few minutes of Pen's increasingly practiced overseeing of their morning wash-up, and getting them properly fed. He was able to foist off all the fish planks on them, since apparently people ate something similar in seaside Raspay, thus acquiring an unearned air of generosity whilst snitching most of the boiled eggs. Godino sat in watchful silence. Pen thought he followed the gist of the murmured Roknari.

Pen supplied him with a brief synopsis of the sisters' misadventures, leaving out his own theological speculations or mention of his magic. "Helping smuggle us aboard some ship bound for Vilnoc or even Lodi would get us out of your temple about as quickly as anything," Pen finished, invitingly.

Godino's "Mm," in reply was unenthusiastic, but not at once negative. With a last injunction to stay quiet, he took himself off to his further temple duties.

More exploration of the harbor town and its other possibilities must wait till dark, Pen conceded, however anxious he was to do *something*, because this island wasn't going to sail itself to Vilnoc.

Soft-voiced language lessons in Cedonian filled some time, till his captive pupils grew mulish.

Then he hit upon letting Des tell stories in Roknari. Not only had six of her ten human riders once been mothers, even Pen hadn't heard all of her two-century stock of memories despite thirteen years of bearing her. Gloomy Umelan in particular was cheered to be called upon. Her clever efforts even won some halting wonder-tales from Jokona in return, which Pen happily stored up. This served much better, as the sun-splashes crept across the floor.

For all of you children, I think, Des murmured fondly.

Pen couldn't muster reproof.

AFTER THREE days trapped in this gentler prison, Pen was growing quietly frantic. A few covert visits to the temple's tiny library provided scant diversion. *Library* was a grandiose description to start with, as it consisted of two scantly filled bookcases sagging against the wall in the old divine's study. When the pirates had ransacked the place, they had carried off anything with fine leather or gilded bindings that might be sold for a high price, leaving only ratty codices protected by thin planks or waxed cloth sewn together with twine, and some tattered scrolls.

Shabby coverings did not necessarily mean that no rare treasure lay hidden within, as Pen was reminded by the example of Jedula Corva, so as he waited for Godino to find help he leafed through every one of them. Despite his diligence he unearthed no sign of his perpetually sought prize of some lost work on sorcery that would teach him more about his craft than he and Des already knew.

Aye, that would be rare indeed, mused Des.

It *could not possibly* be the case that he was—they were—already the most knowledgeable sorcerer-demon pair alive in the world today.

Someone must be, Des pointed out logically.

It can't be me. I still have so many questions!

At least he was able to carry back a couple of simple books written for children in Adriac, and a pair in Cedonian and Roknari, to his young chamber-mates. The well-worn copies were left over from the time when the previous acolyte had taught neighborhood children in the lecture hall, Pen guessed, being religious tales and saints' legends. Some should be lively enough to divert the girls, he hoped, and give point to the language lessons with which, for want of better entertainment, he filled their waking time.

They were probably starting to wonder if he really was a dull scribe, and the alarming *sorcerer* part a self-serving lie like Pozeni's claim to be a divine. He'd so far resisted their urgings to show them some magic, apart from lighting the night-candle, too convenient a skill to forgo. Well, and demonstrating how he'd supplied them with water in the hold, which rendered them gratifyingly wide-eyed. Especially when he followed it up by producing little hailstones, which they held and marveled at and, inevitably, sucked into their mouths and crunched on, grinning.

Benign little tricks, not scary at all. *If you don't think them through.* He could as easily induce an ice ball to form inside a lung, or a testicle. Or, more helpfully, in a tumor, true. But not in a brain, because that would kill at once, laying Des open to repossession by her god. Thus the subtleties of his skills.

Godino's temple kept a cache of donated used garments to be redonated to those in need; Pen supposed he and the girls qualified. It did allow him to cover everyone and then sneak out to the fountain square at night to wash their reeking clothes, a task made easier by a few of Des's surprisingly large stock of small domestic magics. *Well, really, Pen. Ten women. How do you imagine we would not think of these possibilities?* Once he'd learned to access them, he'd found her aids had made his Order's choice of white robes for their learned divines much more manageable. He was starting to miss those robes, and everything that went with them.

Godino brought food and drink faithfully, yes, and bits of news which suggested Pen and his charges were not suspected to still be on this island. But he was inventively elusive about his failure to secure some trusted boatman to ferry them to Vilnoc, or—Pen was getting less fussy—*anywhere* on the opposite coast from which they could at least walk to Vilnoc. Pen began to wonder if Godino was trying to wait them out, induce them to leave on their own from sheer frustration without him ever having to stand up to the menacing sorcerer. Or the menacing pirates. That Pen could perfectly understand his point of view did not make it any less maddening.

The girls, too, grew restive in the enforced quiet, slowly recovering at least physically from their ordeal.

Which, really, had begun with their mother's last illness and hadn't let up yet.

On the fourth night, Pen gritted his teeth and slipped out to make a new survey of the harbor.

IN THE deep dark, the crooked streets of Lanti were deserted by its timid or sober residents, which left only the other sort abroad. Pen had picked out tunic and trousers in a muddled green dye from Godino's stores, and let the girls knot his hair at his nape and tie a black headcloth over it, so at least he didn't glow like the moon in the shadows. As he neared the shore, both Des's Sight and dark-sight allowed him to avoid the late carousers reeling home, and more disturbing sullen shapes curled up in passageways. Not appearing weak to their hungry eyes would fend off the latter, but not being seen at all was better.

He dodged around the warehouses and the customs shed. A cargo-loading crane on heavy wooden wheels was drawn up near the pier by the prison, and Pen quietly climbed it for a better vantage.

Two new ships had arrived and tied up, though whether they were pirates, prizes, or merchants was unclear. The prison was already repopulated, though, and there were a few more guards around it, so at least one vessel must be a prize. In addition to the fire-watch patrolling the shore, crew lingered on board, keeping night-lanterns glimmering orange by the gangplanks. Falun's galley still rode at anchor out in the harbor, so the Rathnattan slaver evidently hadn't filled his quota yet.

I would dearly love to sink that thing, Pen sighed.

I'm for it, Des agreed cheerfully. *Now?*

Tempting. But there might be prisoners chained belowdecks, so it wasn't simply a matter of deploying his favorite sabotages from here. He'd have to swim out, climb aboard, and somehow free them first, multiplying his risks. Not least that of revealing the continuing presence of a sorcerer in Lanti, triggering a serious hunt for him. One ship mysteriously sinking in perfect calm could be put down to any number of causes. Two would start to look decidedly odd.

And the escaping prisoners would still be trapped on this island with their angry captors. Pen was disinclined to sacrifice them for a diversion he did not need.

You're no fun, said Des. If amiably.

He slid down from his perch and slunk off among the piles of fishing gear, nets, and rowboats scattered along the curving strand. Most of the rowboats were meant to ferry crews out to the larger boats at anchor, or fish in the harbor on calm days, and many of them would need at least two strong men to shove them off the sand when the tide was low. A handful of the vessels now moored to buoys out on the lapping water were single-masted craft meant for small crews, so, not impossible; although the smallest craft Pen had ever sailed in on Cedonian seas had carried a crew of three. Hauling up a heavy sail by himself would be a challenge, even with the aid of two wiry girls, though there was a chance there might be some sort of crank for the task.

Could the Corva sisters swim? Most people couldn't, not even, to Pen's surprise, many sailors. The girls would not be very buoyant to tow, though Pen thought he could do it in a pinch.

A splash out on the harbor waters made him flinch, and he peered with both Sight and dark-sight. The inky surface rippled in repeated waves, a faint satin gleam flicking above it. *Ah. Dolphins.* A pod of four or five, it looked like, rolling after one another in pursuit of fish.

Pen wondered if his shamanic persuasion skills, which worked on other animals, would work on dolphins. Or would the blood he would shed in the water as the price of that style of magic just attract sharks? ...Would the persuasion work on sharks? It would be awkward to find out the hard way that it didn't.

Dolphins would be slippery creatures to try to cling to, hard for him, maybe impossible for the girls. So would it be feasible to hitch a dolphin or dolphins to a small boat? How would one devise such a harness? Some sort of yoke or padded ring that would be comfortable for the animal and efficient to get on and off...?

Only you, Pen, said Des, exasperated.

Regretfully, Pen laid the alluring picture of a team of dolphins towing them home to Vilnoc aside for later experimentation, along with his narcoleptic rats. Or only for some dire emergency.

Very unlikely emergency. You are supposed to be selecting a ship to steal, remember?

He hunkered down and studied the inventory. He imagined that the three smallest boats put in and out irregularly about their tasks, but they seemed day-vessels, so likely they were always here at night. One way or another, there should be a boat for him.

He would give Godino one more day to produce better help. If nothing was forthcoming, tomorrow night might be time to take his chances on the unforgiving sea. …Their chances. He grimaced and rose to slither back to the temple.

THE NEXT afternoon, the skies clouded and the wind blew up. Pen found the ladder to the roof and crept around the ledge beneath the clerestory to the top of the portico, lying prone to look out. The height gave him a wide view of both town and harbor. Small boats were hurrying back to their moorings, men rowing ashore with their half-day's catch. Graying wind-waves grew white tops, spume flying from them.

All right, *dead calm* likely wouldn't be helpful for escape either, however much Pen fancied it, but this was too much of a good thing. Pen hissed through his teeth much like the wind, and returned to their hiding-chamber.

He took care to avoid being seen by the temple's few servants, which Godino had described as a groom, a cook-scullion, and a local lad who played acolyte to his divine, equally untutored but valiant in assisting him. Neighborhood women, Pen understood, took it in turns to come to clean and arrange what few flowers or other graces the altars received, before and after ceremonies. Pen and the girls were instructed to lay very low and quiet during these.

That night, the rain rattled the window lattice in gusts. Pen cursed in Wealdean, rolled over, and went back to sleep.

THE DELAY was repaid to him the next day when Godino slipped in to announce he had secured a willing ferryman.

"Safe and secret?" asked Pen.

Godino shrugged. "Jato, I trust. He vouches for his crew."

"You did let him know there will be some reward to compensate them for their risks when we reach Vilnoc?" And, with luck, something to send back to Godino.

"Of course. They aren't fellows who can afford charity. Or defiance, so if the risks come down on them, the reward won't be much use. Keep that in mind, Learned."

True enough, so Pen didn't quibble. "How soon can we leave?"

"On tomorrow afternoon's tide."

"In broad daylight?" Pen frowned.

"It will be the busiest time. And look less suspicious than putting out at night."

"Hm, I suppose." However uncertain Godino's selection was, it still had to be better than Pen trying to find a boatman blind, with no local knowledge. "I trust you have not told him I'm a sorcerer."

"He wouldn't have agreed to take you if I had."

"What did you tell him?"

"That you were a man who wanted to go in secret to Vilnoc."

"Not that we were escaped captives?"

"No, not that either, for the same reason, though I don't doubt he figures something smells. But if you think that him pleading he didn't know would save him from Guild reprisals, you're more optimistic than either of us."

Godino offloaded their lunch and swapped out their chamber pot. Pen wondered how private the man had really managed to keep his unwanted guests from the other temple servants. The non-arrival of some gang of rowdies to recapture them—well, try to—was the only clue Pen had, though it did suggest the temple people were either very loyal, or still in ignorance.

I approve of ignorance, Des commented. *It cannot fuel betrayal.*

"What did Brother Godino say?" Lencia asked anxiously when the door had closed behind the man.

"He was talking about boats, wasn't he?" said tense Seuka, sitting up. "Did he get us a boat to go on?"

"Yes, and boatmen," replied Pen. "I was preparing to steal one two nights ago, but this is safer. Bigger." And without a novice at the tiller. "Plus I won't have to deprive some poor honest fisherman of his livelihood. There are few enough honest men on Lantihera."

He wondered if he should try to arm the sisters. Knives of a size they could handle wouldn't be much use against a war hammer, even in trained hands. Their thin safety lay in their sale value, which was not high. It wouldn't take much resistance for an assailant to decide they weren't worth the aggravation and move on to easy murders. Pirates quite preferred weak opponents. Still… "Shall I try to get you some belt knives from Godino?"

"Yes!" said Seuka.

But Lencia looked at him more coolly. "You don't have one."

"It was taken from me the first day. I usually used it for shaping quills."

"Knives would be better than nothing," she conceded.

Pen was by no means sure. But it might make them feel better, and so just that hair less likely to panic in a tight moment. "I'll see what I can get."

Pen continued to think out loud while sharing around the flatbread and goat cheese. "Packing won't be a problem. Nor water, though we'd best keep that trick out of sight of our crew. It might be well to persuade Godino to give us a little food for the voyage. Which should be short." His heart clenched in the hope he'd been strangling since his capture as too distracting. "We could be home in as little as three days."

He'd only lived a year in Vilnoc, so he wasn't really homesick for the town. It was their narrow house, or rather, its occupants—Nikys, her mother Idrene, yes, even her brother Adelis. He wasn't sure if he'd made them his family, or they'd made him theirs, but either way, they were the new and unanticipated anchor for his life's wandering vessel.

The girls were giving him their wary looks again, reminding him that this proposed destination wasn't home to them, but rather, another alien waystation in their uprooted existences. Just another strange place where strange grownups would be disposing of their lives, more benevolently than slavers but giving them as little choice.

Pen launched into a description of his house, and its back courtyard common with its row, his quiet, book-rich study, and of Nikys and Idrene, with the notion of giving the sisters a share of his hope. Though their questions led promptly away, through his account of Nikys's charge who was just Seuka's age, to a description of the high ducal household. This seemed to fascinate them more, as if it were a wonder-tale like the ones they'd been sharing the other day. Pen could remember feeling that way as a lad, reading stories of brave nobles in faraway places, though any lingering wonder had been stripped out of him by close service to three successive courts. He did not hurry to disillusion them.

SOON AFTER noon the next day, Godino sent his servants on errands and conducted Pen and the girls to the side entry by the stable. His friend—or so Pen hoped—Jato was leaning against the gatepost with his burly arms crossed, scuffing his sandal in the dirt. The red-brick tone of his sunburn suggested Cedonian ancestry, set off by black hair and beard trimmed short. He wore the common garb of a common sailor, sleeveless shirt and calf-length trousers, sash and belt and knife. He glanced up frowning as they approached.

Pen had attempted to reduce his excessive recognizability by tying his queue in a knot again, and topping his pale head with a worn and stained straw hat. And slouching. He wore the local muddled greens, for whatever use that was. The girls, after a long debate over Godino's proffered cast-offs, had dressed themselves as boys. Lencia's dark curls barely went into a queue, and Seuka's ruddy tangle had needed to be forcibly restrained, but altogether they made a passable pair of street rats, hardly worth anyone's second glance. Certainly they little resembled an escaped Lodi scribe and his two nieces.

Jato looked them over. "Vilnoc, eh?"

Pen touched his hat brim. "If you will. You'll be paid as soon after our safe arrival as I can arrange it."

"Huh." Without further comment, Jato pushed off from the gatepost and motioned them after him. Godino closed his gate with a noisy sigh of relief. Under Jato's eyes Pen couldn't sign a grateful formal blessing as befit a learned divine, but he thought it, tapping his fingers and hoping the gods would know.

The girls started to reach for Penric's hands, but then caught themselves and strode out at his sides more boy-like, fists clenched near their new-old belt knives. He gave them both approving nods and followed Jato in equal silence into the winding streets, not letting his stride lengthen unduly. He could hardly wait to get off this island.

Be on your guard now more than ever, came a murmuring in his head that Pen recognized as Umelan, and not just by her Archipelago idiom. *There remains that very common way to slay a sorcerer by luring him into a boat with promises of succor or pleasure or transport, sailing out some miles, and then throwing him overboard and sailing off before he drowns and his demon jumps. It was how my clan tried to kill me, after Mira's death in Lodi both released and bound me.* The keening grief of that long-ago betrayal still resonated in her bodiless voice. *I, too, had thought I was going home.*

I am advised, Pen promised her. Almost the only way to kill a sorcerer of any experience was by subterfuge and surprise, really. But Jato, at least, didn't flinch from him, bore no tension suggesting he planned such an ambush, showed no more caution than expected toward any chancy passenger.

The passers-by, at this hour, were largely women and servants going to or from the markets, or carrying water jars, who gave them only enough notice to gauge their harmlessness. At length, they debouched from the alleys about midway between the two piers.

Beside a heavy rowboat drawn up on the sand, four men waited, idly leaning against the thwart or crouching in its thin shade. They stood up, and one waved, as Jato and his tail trod down to them.

They shuffled to a halt, and Jato looked over his crew. "Where're the other two?"

"They said they'd be along soon," replied the man who'd waved. They looked a typical array of Lanti seamen, dressed like their captain, with a mixed range of skin and hair color, leathery rather than bulky, none as tall as Pen. The crewman looked off tensely up the shore. Too tensely.

Pen followed his glance and thought Wealdean words. Apparently, he wasn't even going to have to wait till they were at sea for betrayal.

A dozen men trotted toward them. All but two wore the tabards of the port guards, and were erratically armed with short swords, long knives, a couple of pikes, two crossbows and two short bows. Had that wave been a signal? By Jato's jerk and curse, this delegation was a surprise to him too, and to three of the four other men at his side.

It wasn't hard to follow the logic. If his crewmen followed Jato, they might be rewarded later in Vilnoc, but if they betrayed him here, they would be rewarded right now, more certainly and with less effort. In addition to whatever bounty the Guild offered for the return of escaped slaves, if Jato came to a bad end because of this they might even expect to receive his ship as a prize.

"Stay behind me and stick tight," Pen told the girls, who, watching in horror, hardly needed the instruction. "Things are about to get messy."

The port guards spread out, expecting sensible surrender in the face of the odds. Jato and two of his three loyalists drew together, although the other stepped back with his hands raised, glumly anticipating events.

One thing was plain. While clearly someone had figured out Pen's party were fugitive captives, no one had yet realized he was also the sorcerer who had blasted through the prison the night the *Autumn's Hand* had escaped. Or they would have brought a couple of hundred rowdies to try to take him, not just a dozen.

The guard leader stepped forward. "Give it up, Jato," he advised genially. "You can't fight us all. Besides, we know where you den up."

By Jato's flinch, Pen wondered if the man had a family.

Bastard's *teeth* but Pen was getting tired of this. And tired in general, and homesick, and *angry. You know...* he thought to Des. *Let's just get started.*

Something like a purr sounded in the back of his mind. Did lionesses purr?

No, smirked Des. *But chaos demons might.*

Almost perfunctorily, Pen snapped the four bowstrings. Distance weapons summarily disposed of, next most dangerous were the pikes and their bearers, then the swords and knives. And fists and boots.

With enemies this numerous, efficiency was going to be required. No time for pretty tricks. The magic to destroy all those weapons would be an unaffordable drain. That left the wielders. *But not for long.*

Pen began picking out and ruffling big sciatic nerves, hard, starting with the nearest men. His victims discovered this the first time they started to step forward, and instead fell or staggered, shrieking in surprise and pain. It took a minute of close concentration to work through the entire dozen.

A gasp of surprise brought his attention around. Jato's eyes were rimmed white. "You're that sorcerer!"

No denying it now. "Well, yes, but no danger to you. We can still escape." Pen gave the rowboat a shove. It didn't budge. "The four of us, plus me, should still manage to sail. Hurry!"

Jato did hurry—choosing to pelt away along the sand, trailed by his remaining men.

"Bastard piss on you for cowards!" Pen yelled after them, uselessly.

He wheeled, urgently surveying the harbor for other, smaller boats, and smaller rowboats to get out to them. The three likely candidates he'd picked out the other night were gone fishing or whatever, their owners making good use of this bright sailing

day, their ferries tethered out at the moorings await-
ing their return. Nothing else lay within immediate
rowing or even swimming distance, though a couple
more full-sized probably-pirate ships had recently
arrived to drop anchor and await their turn at the
loaded piers.

A yelp from behind him and Lencia's scream of
"Seuka!" whipped him around again.

Pen had overlooked one man, the crewman who
had made to surrender first. For whatever reason,
he'd chosen to grab up Seuka and start running for
the town. Seizing the potential reward? Planning
to offer her to the Guild as an apology in hopes of
gaining a pardon? Saving her from the evil sorcerer?
Pen couldn't guess, but the son of a bitch was *fast*,
even with Seuka struggling and kicking in his grip.

Worse, Lencia had started running after them.

"Lencia, stop!" Pen cried at her, and was unsurprisingly ignored. "*Sunder* it!" He clenched his teeth
and sprinted in pursuit, his straw hat blowing off.

The kidnapper, or rescuer, angled up through the
shore clutter. Pen overtook Lencia, her legs churning and her face set in a determined grimace, and
did not stop. Moving targets were harder to hit with
the delicate but so-effective internal disruptions, and

this fellow was no exception. Furious as Pen was, he wasn't furious enough to risk death and Des.

He didn't have to. About the time the crewman swung in past the warehouse near the prison-side customs shed, Seuka finally managed to get a hand on her belt knife, draw it, and poke at her captor. He barked more in surprise than pain, but flung her aside reflexively. She slammed into the whitewashed wall and slid down. The fellow started to reach for her again, but then looked over his shoulder at Pen wrathfully closing upon him, jolted in fear, abandoned his prize, and just ran.

Pen let him go. He stopped, gasping, by Seuka, who was sitting up shakily not-crying.

"Are you all right?"

"Yes," she sniffled, breathlessly. No broken bones, at least, as there might have been. Bruises would show later.

Lencia arrived in their wake, also winded and not-crying, or at least denying the smears evaporating on her flushed cheeks. "Seuka, you idiot! Why did you let him grab you?"

"I didn't *let* him. He just did!"

Pen turned back to survey what was happening on the beach. Quite a lot, regrettably, as people hurried to and away from the men he'd left in moaning heaps near Jato's rowboat. The hunt would be up in minutes, and this time, he suspected, they would not repeat the mistake of trying to take him on with insufficient numbers.

Better give them something else to worry about.

Des, what do you make of the contents of this warehouse?

Crammed. Bolts of cloth, piles of clothes, furniture, all sorts of miscellaneous thievings. Plaster floor but wooden roof. The impression of an edged smile. *Very dry.*

Do it.

Yes, Penric, love.

He braced one arm against the wall and leaned, enduring the ripple of heat that even the most downhill of magics generated in his body. And this was going to be very downhill indeed.

Enough. Let the white god's fire do its own work. An offering to make up for that cold temple plinth.

Right. Saving room for dessert, my lord.

A grin snaked over his face. Des only used his old title when she was exceptionally pleased with him.

"On your feet, now," he told Seuka, giving her a hand up. She rose easily, so thin and light. No wonder her would-be stealer had made good time. "Follow me. Let's go around the back of this building." Temporarily out of sight from the shore, though more than one person must have seen where they'd run to.

They skated along the side facing the town, passing a locked double door. Pen kicked it open in passing to provide a better draft for his soon-to-be furnace. He paused at the corner. From the next building over, the customs shed, a few men ran off to investigate the uproar going on down by Jato's rowboat. Pen led the girls past the rearward side of the long shed, trailing his hand over the planks, feeling each little back-blow of heat, *magical friction* Learned Ruchia had dubbed it. Dry wood indeed.

Next over was the prison. A half-dozen guards on the roof were gathered gazing out under the flats of their hands, also toward the shore. Pen considered efficiencies. *Moving fast* wasn't going to be useful for much longer, but he thought he might squeeze one more foray out of it.

Leaving the sisters next to a building that would shortly be ablaze wouldn't do, so he took their hands to prevent straying and had them hunker down by the corner of the prison, holding his finger to his lips to enjoin silence. He walked around to the back entry where, this time, two guards were posted, leaning against the stone wall but otherwise alert. Reaching for their short swords, they both pushed off and scowled at Pen's smile as he approached with both his hands held out empty. For a moment, poised to react, they were usefully still.

Lingual nerves, sciatic nerves, axillary nerves, brush, brush, brush, and they were down, choking and writhing. He stepped around them and down the steps, lifted the bar, and popped the bolt. A quick jog down the dark central corridor left every lock hanging open. He pushed his head into the main prison, just as full of unhappy men as it had been the other night, and was there no *end* to this trade, and called in Adriac, "The rear doors are open. What you do with that fact is up to you."

He hurried back out to where the girls stood staring down in shocked fascination at the guards he'd dropped.

"Was *that* a magic spell?" asked Lencia.

"No. Well, not technically. I really don't think of anything other than a shamanic persuasion or geas as a *spell*, exactly." They scrunched their brows at him, disbelievingly. "I'll teach you the distinctions sometime if you're interested, when we get home. But first we have to get home. *This* way."

They continued on from the prison. Pen did not look back as the first hoarse voices reached the back doors and grew louder, fearfully marveling. Some of those men might die in this escape attempt, but… not by his hand.

You can't save everyone, Pen, Des consoled him.

Yes. I learned that well back in Martensbridge. I am not likely to forget.

He was flushed with heat, sweat tricking down his neck and back. The next building seemed to be a run-down taverna. A couple of servants idling by its back door stared at him and the girls as they trotted past, but did not attempt to impede them, their attention seized by the outflux of men from the prison. They hastily darted back inside and barred their door, shouting warnings. Pen led the girls around the far side of the dingy building to where he could again get a view of the harbor.

The crane he'd climbed the other day had been moved out to the pier, probably by an ox team, and was engaged in either loading or unloading one of the ships. The stevedores had dropped their work and were shouting and pointing back up the shore toward the warehouse and customs shed, from which dark gray smoke was now billowing, its nose-stinging acridity already penetrating the soft salt air. Most of them abandoned the pier and jogged off toward the fires. Pen expected some sort of bucket brigade from the sea would soon be organized. He didn't think they'd be able to save either building, but they were welcome to try.

His feet were still planted on this bloody island. *Ships. Boats. Rowboats. Rafts, barrels, anything.*

Out in the harbor beyond the pier, Falun's galley still sat. Pen hadn't had much luck with the gratitude of freed prisoners up to now, but being chained in the hold of such a ship must surely concentrate the mind. Given the choice of rowing to Rathnatta and slavery, or Vilnoc and freedom, surely he wouldn't have to apply much persuasion...? He could probably swim out that far, but—

"Do you see any rowboats at all?" Pen asked the girls, squinting.

Lencia stood on tiptoe. "There! In the shadows under the pier."

"Ah. Yes. Well, it's our rowboat now. Come on!"

In the clash between terror and excitement, excitement must be winning, for they followed him all-eagerness, laughing a bit wildly. They slid down and clambered awkwardly over the stones at the shaded base of the jetty. The boat's painter was hitched to a rusty iron ring driven into one of the big boulders. Pen waded without hesitation into the murky water laced with tan foam. It wasn't cold by his standards—in the *cantons*, you could drive a horse and sleigh across *properly* cold water—but it was cooler than his body, and drew dangerous heat from his blood. He ducked his head for good measure, then shoved the boat around close enough for the girls to tumble in.

Oars lay tucked under the thwarts. Pen was more surprised by their presence than he would have been by their absence, at this point. He might have swum ahead towing the boat by its rope, he supposed, much like his imagined dolphin, but it would have been slow going. He unhitched the knot, heaved a leg inboard, and shoved off, flopping down into the damp bottom where he lay wheezing for a moment.

The girls must have been in a rowboat before— well, Raspay was a port town—because they earnestly pulled up the heavy oars and managed to get their pins seated in their oarlocks without dropping one overboard. Then they looked to Pen.

"Where are we going?" asked Lencia. "We can't row to Vilnoc."

"Alas, no. Just out to that galley." Pen gestured. "You boys can row if you want."

"Oh!" Seuka grinned in delight, and the two hastily arranged themselves on one seat, an oar each. They pulled with reasonable coordination, and the boat began to slowly move alongside the ship docked on this side, its hull rising up like a wooden wall.

A head and shoulders leaned over the top of this bulwark. "Hey!" shouted the silhouette. "What are you doing?"

Good question. Pen wished he knew the answer. He crawled over to the side of their boat, propped his chin on the thwart, and considered the passing hull. Running a dual line of rot along it just below the waterline for several yards as they rowed by seemed almost routine, but he wasn't above trying anything. He wasn't sure if he was about to sink a pirate, a prize, or a legitimate merchant, and at this point scarcely cared.

Des *giggled*. She was getting dangerously excited much like the girls, but he couldn't bleed off her nervous energy with rowing.

As they came out into the sunlight and the view widened, he rolled over on his back and studied the rigging of the ship tied up on the far side of the dock. Almost out of range, he snapped stays and started a couple of fires in the rolled-up sails. "The Bastard's blessings upon you all," he murmured, and bit his thumb at them.

Lencia gave him a chary look. Seuka, intent upon her rowing, just sucked her lip in concentration.

Pen considered his next plan. It was probable that most of Falun's crew were enjoying time ashore, though some might be engaged with provisioning. Prisoners, even if chained, required some guards. He was getting very practiced with guards, but that was no invitation to get careless. He was also hot and ragged and worried, with red anger pulsing treacherously through his veins, but dwelling on any of those things was no help. He hoisted himself upright and squinted at the galley.

"I think I see climbing netting hanging over the port side. Row over that way."

They passed not far from another vessel at anchor, clearly a rich pirate by its sleek lines and three masts prepared to carry a wide burden of sails for speed. Some crewmen hung on its landward-side rail, pointing and goggling at the clawing blazes ashore, the flames a strange transparent orange in the bright daylight, the air above them shimmering. Pen systematically snapped every stay within his range, igniting the rigging as it collapsed. Cries turned to screams.

There *was* crew aboard the galley, ah, for they, too, had collected on the starboard side to watch the inexplicable disaster progress. Visible smoke was finally rising from the pier. The hull Pen had perforated was starting to list, ever so gently, outward.

Two boys and a man plodding along in a little rowboat passed unremarked, with all this show going on.

"Isn't this Captain Falun's slave galley?" asked Lencia apprehensively as they slid into the shade of its far side.

"Ayup," said Pen, discarding his wet, worn, stolen sandals as slippery and useless. He sat up and prepared to reach for the netting.

"Isn't that *dangerous?*"

"Probably," sighed Pen. "I think I'm getting used to it." He looked up past the line of oar ports, back at the girls. "Stay here a few paces off, and be ready to row away if they start to come for you."

They looked at each other. "Without you?" said Seuka in a tentative voice.

"If necessary."

Lencia cocked her head at him, and said in a remarkably dry tone for a ten-year-old, "To where?"

Pen stared around the disrupted harbor. "I'll... return."

"You'd better," said Seuka, with determination.

Pen swung up onto the coarse rope weave and flashed a grin over his shoulder. "I thought I was the evil sorcerer."

Lencia shot back, "Yes, but you're *our* evil sorcerer."

"Ah." Pen hung a moment, liminally, letting that claim settle into his bones. It made him feel oddly fond. "Yes. I think that must be so."

Seuka nodded firmly. "So don't you get hacked up, either."

"I'll do all I can." He hesitated, then corrected that to, "All we can." Because whatever he was heading into, he wasn't going alone. He tapped his lips with his thumb, felt for toeholds, and pushed himself up the side.

I told you I liked those girls, said Des smugly.

You were right. He paused just before mounting the deck. *Sight.* No souls immediately nearby, though that didn't mean someone farther off couldn't be looking this way. He rolled silently over the rail and crouched barefoot, taking his bearings.

He was on a kind of walkway between the rail and one of the two low sheds or cabins that filled the deck fore and aft on either side of the mainmast. This galley was square-rigged in an older style, though with a smaller mast toward the bow for some sort of jib sail that had the air of a later addition. Somewhere, there must be hatches down to holds... there. He edged around the cabin, found the dark square in the deck, and slithered down something like a lethal cross between a stairway and a ladder.

Headroom was scant, he found out by barking his scalp. This space seemed devoted to cargo and crew quarters, judging by the hammocks tucked here and there. Down again. This was the oar deck, oval beams of sunlight from the ports dotting the deck and benches in a row, the glimmer of wave reflections dancing over the low ceiling, a surprising lack of stench. And one more descent, into unrelieved shadow; his dark-sight came up without thought, laying his surroundings bare. *This* was the hold for Falun's lucrative human cargo. Pen could tell by the long rows of leg irons bolted to the hull braces.

Empty. Falun hadn't loaded on yet.

Bastard blast it, I could have sunk this accursed ship the other night!

Pen fell to his knees in something not quite a prayer. *Lord god Bastard, I dedicate this day to you. I hope you are suitably amused. In fact, you can have this whole detestable week...*

Apart from two sisters waiting in hope for him out on the water. Pen was keeping that godly gift. That being so, falling over in a lump of rage and despair and drumming his heels on the deck like some uncannily dangerous two-year-old was not an option.

Preferably not, murmured Des. *You know we old mothers have tricks for dealing with such tantrums.*

I'd rather not find out.

He sighed and clambered back to his feet, and up the ladder-stairs. No prisoner-crew to conscript. A ship too big for him to sail. What next?

If you start pining after those dolphins again, said Des, *I'm going to slap you.*

Pen's lips twitched up despite everything. *What, I think it's a grand idea...*

Pen stepped up into the light to discover that what was next was Captain Falun exiting the door from the aft cabin and stopping short, staring at him in astonishment. "You!"

Pen scratched his scalp, damp and sticky and itchy with seawater. "You know," he said conversationally in high Roknari—the mode of scholar to servant was nicely insulting—"I've been having an extraordinarily aggravating day. You probably shouldn't *add* to it."

Falun didn't listen, of course. People seldom did. Instead he started back and drew a sharp cutlass from a rack on the cabin wall, turned, and lunged at Pen.

Pen sheared the complex conglomeration of nerves in his armpit clean in half. Falun's arm fell limply and hung at his side, the cutlass falling from suddenly lifeless fingers to clatter on the deck. "*What...?*" He stumbled, unbalanced, the arm swinging from his shoulder like a heavy sack, confusingly painless.

He'd never be lifting a sword again. Or a spoon.

"I could do the same thing to the nerves from your eyes, you know," Pen informed him. "It wouldn't even be theologically forbidden."

For all his dapper air, Falun didn't keep captive slaves in line, or control the rowdies who kept them in line for him, by being kindly or slow. He bellowed and bent and grabbed for the cutlass with his working hand. Pen danced back from the rising slash and scraped Falun's sciatic nerves good and hard, and then he went down and didn't get up.

The noise, of course, drew his crew away from the distractions at the railing, plus a servant-or-slave from the cabin, and then Pen was put to putting all of *them* down. Fortunately, there were only half-a-dozen men aboard at present, and their mystification at what was happening gave Pen a marginal advantage which he used to the full.

He surveyed the resultant heap of humanity, flopping around at his feet like a catch of fish. He *could* shove them all overboard into the harbor to drown like a betrayed sorcerer. He could. At least physically. Theologically borderline, such murders, hurrying souls unripe to their gods.

Instead he stepped over the groaning bodies to the base of the mainmast and looked up. A line of pegs for gripping, a crow's nest at the top. Des whimpered.

Yes, yes. The ship is barely rocking. Endure, love. He stretched and climbed, realizing about halfway up just how exhausted he was when his arms started shaking. Des whimpered some more, but he made it up to the bare perch of the lookout without falling, wrapped his legs around the last of the mast, and clung.

He first checked for the Corva sisters in their rowboat. There they were, still bobbing about in the shade of the galley. He waved. They waved back, upturned faces puzzled but reassured.

Next, he swiveled around to observe the shore.

Goodness, said Des. One might take the remark for surprise, but to Pen it sounded more like glee.

Three columns of black smoke boiled skyward, blending in the upper air, one from the warehouse, one from the customs shed, and one from the pier. The two docked ships and their pier were all afire now. Well, one ship was having a conflict between rising water and descending flames. Pen wasn't sure if fire or water would win, but it was plain the ship was going to lose. In all three locations, people had given up running around yelling and hauling buckets, and just stood back in little groups watching in morbid consternation.

The rich pirate ship nearby was not faring fortunately either, or else was coming along quite well depending on one's point of view. Pen thought it was lovely, and so, by her approving hum, did Des. The fire had spread from the collapsed rigging to the deck and below, and the sailors were in process of abandoning it, crowded into a teetering rowboat or swimming with the aid of planks or spars tossed overboard.

Pen studied his trail of chaos. *We aren't going to be welcome back in Lanti, are we.*

Shouldn't think it, no, agreed Des.

That's fine. I didn't like the town anyway.

Pen blew out his breath and started looking around the harbor for something, anything, that floated, had a sail, and was smaller than a whale. They now possessed a rowboat to get to it, so they were that much to the good after all this effort. With all his running, had he only succeeded in running them into a blind alley?

A wink of light and flash of color at the broad harbor mouth drew his attention away from the spectacle of the shore, and he swung around and squinted.

It was a galley. The color had been a sail being furled, the light a reflection off the long double bank of wet oars as they rose and dipped, turning the ship in toward the town. Another Roknari slaver? No, too narrow, too swift…

That's a war galley, said Des. She couldn't sit bolt upright in alarm, but Pen could rise for both of them, standing on the support and peering out under the edge of his hand.

No...not a war galley... One, two, three...six, with others occluded behind, seven, nine, ten... A couple of fat freight cogs sailed after, the nautical equivalent of a baggage train. The Carpagamons finally coming to reclaim their island? Some Rathnattan prince doing the same? The ships were actually more in the Cedonian style of current naval architecture.

A breath of breeze in the mild afternoon blew the lead ship's pennants out straight.

...What was half the duke of Orbas's fleet doing *here?*

And, oh yes, Pen recognized the commander's banner. Nikys had painstakingly and lovingly sewn it for her dear brother, after all.

General Adelis Arisaydia, scourge of the Rusylli and pride and terror of his troops. Pride because terror, Pen gathered, because soldiers thought like that.

He sat with his mouth hanging open and watched in stunned fascination as the Orban fleet paraded into Lanti Harbor.

IN ANOTHER moment, Pen overcame his paralysis and scrambled down the mast so fast it made Des yip. He pounded across the deck, leaping the groaning, swearing bodies who had not yet begun to find their feet, and thrust his head over the rail.

"Lencia! Seuka! Come get me, quickly!"

Alarmed, the girls rowed near as Pen swung out onto the netting and dropped into the boat, making it dip and pitch. "I'll take the oars now."

"Are they after you?" asked Seuka, with a fierce look up at Falun's galley.

"No, but I need to catch my brother-in-law."

"What?" said Lencia, giving up her seat to Pen's urgency. "...You have a brother-in-law?"

"Yes, and he's here. Somehow." The boat surged as Pen dug in the oars. He only had time to blast a few fist-sized patches of rot below Falun's waterline in passing, which did not nearly relieve his feelings.

As they rounded the slaver, Pen glanced over his shoulder and tried to select a course that would intercept the flagship. Unfairly, Adelis had far more oars than he did, but then the general—or was he appointed an admiral for this venture?—also had a boat measured in tons. Many tons. With great momentum, and a bronze rostrum that could rip through enemy hulls even faster than Pen could.

And, if those ships were full of his seasoned Rusylli-campaign veterans, he led a gang of brutes who could eat pirate rowdies for lunch, and possibly intended to.

As the two vessels converged, Pen stood up on his knees on his seat, shouted, and waved frantically. Lookouts observed, conferred; in a moment, a broad, tough, familiar figure in an army cuirass of boiled leather plates and a thrown-back red cloak came to the rail, saw him, and called orders over his shoulder. After a moment, all the churning oars rose in unison and paused. Men hurried, and a climbing net was flung over the bow ahead of the oar banks.

Pen rowed faster, the ship slowed, and he managed to bump the rowboat into the right spot. "Grab on!" he yelled at the girls, who reached for the netting. They didn't quite match speed before they were pulled out right over the thwart; Pen hastily followed, ready to lunge or if necessary dive for a falling young body, but they clung on and climbed. The rowboat thunked off the hull and spun away, and Pen spared a hope its poor owner would eventually find it.

Many strong arms reached down to pull them up and inboard, and Pen in turn. "Ah!" Clutching the rail, he hauled himself to his feet and looked around.

Boots clumped across the deck, and Adelis stood before him, hands on his hips, shaking his head in exasperation. "There you are. Why am I not even surprised?"

"However did you know where to find me?"

"I thought the columns of smoke were a good guide."

"Well, yes, but—" Pen became aware of the sisters shrinking to his sides, staring in fear at Adelis.

Pen didn't find Adelis in the least fearful, but then, he was used to him. Muscular build, Cedonian brick-colored skin, black hair in a military cut, clean shaved, all very normal up to the top half of his face. There, severe red and white burn scars framed his eyes in a pattern like an owl's feathers. His irises were a strange deep garnet color, glowing like coals under the black mantel of his eyebrows when the light caught them. Pen knew every inch of that face, since he'd healed it after the murderous boiling acid that had been meant to steal Adelis's sight permanently. That Adelis had smoothly refitted both miraculous recovery and horrifying scars into support of his commander's reputation was all Adelis, though.

Pen granted the effect was a bit shocking when one first encountered it. He didn't think his brother-in-law would enjoy little girls screaming at the sight of him, though, so he hurried his introductions, first in Roknari, of which Adelis had a good working grasp.

"Lencia, Seuka, this is my wife's twin brother, General Adelis Arisaydia." Pen made his voice deliberately cheerful, by way of guidance. "He serves the duke of Orbas, as Nikys and I do."

Well, not quite the same way, suggested Adelis's eyebrow twitch.

Switching to Cedonian, "Adelis, this is Lencia and Seuka Corva, late of Raspay, orphans and wards of my Order. And so of me, for the moment. I haven't been able to teach them much Cedonian yet, though we're working on it."

"Ah," said Adelis. He looked down wryly at the sisters. In passable low Roknari, he said, "Welcome to my flagship the *Eye of Orbas*, Lencia and Seuka Corva. How did you come to meet our Penric?"

"He...dropped from the sky?" Seuka offered hesitantly.

"The pirates threw him into the hold where we were prisoners," Lencia clarified this. "Then we were all brought to Lantihera and sold, and we've been trying to get away ever since."

"It's a long tale that I can tell later," said Pen. The merest glance confirmed Adelis had his hands full right now, from the anxious officers clustered around him like bees tending their queen to the trail of ships following on their stern, signal flags flapping. "But—how did you chance to come to Lantihera? Do you mean to conquer the island?"

"Brother of Autumn avert, no." Adelis tapped his fist over his heart in unironic prayer. "It's much too far from Orbas's coast to defend, and has no strategic value to us. Quite the reverse. We don't need to let them know that, though." A sardonic jerk of his head toward the burning waterfront. "But the Lanti pirates have been annoying Orbas for some time. Yours was the third Orban ship captured this year, and they lately raided a village on Pulpi." One of the dukedom's few coastal islands. "Duke Jurgo was fed up, so he sent me to persuade them to stop."

Along with a couple thousands of his friends, evidently.

"He granted me discretion as to how. Extracting you, which I figured for the trickiest part, is unexpectedly accomplished. And razing the town in revenge for you seems...redundant. Is that chaos all your doing?"

"More or less." Penric rubbed his tired, smoke-stung, itching eyes. "It's been a bad day."

"I see that." Adelis tilted his head, lightened his tone. "And do I also find you well, Madame Desdemona?"

"Yes, indeed, General," said Des through Pen's mouth, which he politely yielded to her. "I'm having a delightful outing."

A scimitar glint slipped across Adelis's mouth. Initially appalled, Adelis had only gradually become reconciled to Penric's demon, but lately he'd begun to treat her as a sort of invisible sister-in-law. It was their shared bloody-mindedness that had finally broken the ice, Pen decided.

"But," said Penric. "How did you even know I was here?"

Adelis snorted. "First was that ship you'd boarded in Trigonie, which sailed into Vilnoc complaining of their mishandling. Its crew had retaken it in the night, and it probably arrived not long after you reached Lantihera—though the description of their missing passenger took about a day to reach anyone who actually knew what you were. Next was your travel-box, which some fishermen had hauled up in their nets and couldn't get open, so brought to Nikys. Who did not react well." Adelis grimaced. "Third was an Adriac merchanter with damaged water casks and a lurid tale of their escape in which you featured almost, but not quite, unrecognizably. Once is happenstance. Twice is coincidence. Three times begins to seem like a message to be ignored at one's peril." He cleared his throat. "And Nikys, of course. Very upset. Also to be ignored at one's peril."

"Oh," said Penric. Warmed. Disturbed, but also warmed.

Adelis rubbed the back of his neck and huffed. "Fishing you out of the harbor first upends my tactical plans. Not that they aren't always. Eh, but I think I can do something interesting with this." He didn't look very discommoded.

He motioned over a beardless young officer and detailed him to escort Penric and the Corva sisters to his own cabin. "Get them whatever they need."

The lad led Penric and his charges off, picking their way over the deck. Adelis, gesturing, was the brief center of a new flurry, men departing this way and that, more signal flags urgently rising. Handling ships, Pen reflected, seemed a much more complicated matter than sinking them. But at least he seemed unlikely to be tossed overboard from this one.

ADELIS'S CABIN, tucked down in a corner by the stern, proved an even smaller closet than the coffin on Pen's first ship. It did feature a solid bunk, not a hammock, which was soon put to use with its fold-down board as table for the basin and wash-water the aide brought at Pen's earnest request, plus food or at least rations. Pen gave the girls their pick and then, famished to the point of tremors, snacked on olives, rather stale bread rounds, dried fruit, cheese curds, more olives, and even ate his fish plank.

He and Des personally supplied much purer drinking water all around, worth the heat-price, taming the harsh red army wine. Everyone frugally shared basin, soap chunk, and washrag, and Pen sacrificed the last of the limited ewer of cask-water to lather and rinse his crusting hair.

Clean sailors' tunics, belted with braided cord, made neat modest dresses for the girls, though they made it plain they meant to preserve their boys' togs as precious plunder. Pen did not miss the tunic and trousers he'd been captured in, not new to start with and last seen much worse for wear, but he wondered how soon the girls would realize the sack of food and clothes they had lost when attacked on the beach included the last work of their mother's hands.

About to redon, with distaste, the damp, muddled-green cast-offs, Pen was startled when the aide brought out and handed him a neat bundle of his own clothes from Vilnoc.

"Madame Nikys sent them with the general," the young officer informed him proudly. "She had great faith in him."

Fine linen drawers. Slim tan trousers. The summer tunic of his rank and Order: sleeveless pale linen, its high neck supported by the silver-plated torc that was the only uncomfortable bit of it. Split down the sides from the hips, it fell to his calves in two panels, slits and hems weighted with a band embroidered with a frieze of creatures sacred to the Bastard in Orbas: rats and crows, gulls and hill vultures, some ambiguous insects, all much more endearing than in real life. It was cinched with a braided sash intertwining white and cream, proclaiming his rank as a senior divine, and its third strand of silver marking, or perhaps warning of, his status as a Temple sorcerer.

Every stitch of it lovingly spun, woven, and sewn by Nikys. Putting it on was like easing into her embrace. It also allowed him to slip in a small lesson in Quintarian theology to the girls, intrigued by its meaningful details but mostly taken with the cavorting needlework creatures.

His rank and calling seemed to settle again on his shoulders with his garb; not inwardly, whence it never strayed, but certainly outwardly, judging by the way the aide stepped back half a pace in new respect. Or possibly caution.

Good, purred Des. *About time we received our due.*

No furious fighting had erupted outside, obviously. Pen had heard the rattle of the ship's stone anchor being let down a while ago, the very opposite of rowing like mad to ram some doomed target. Had there been any left.

Adelis, he shortly learned when they ventured back out onto the deck, had gone ashore for a parley with whatever quorum of the Guild and the town council could be hastily gathered. He'd trailed an honor guard of a few hundred sturdy, heavily armed soldiers. The rest of the fleet hovered on the water, temporarily quiescent but alert. Any lesser Lanti vessels had scattered away like frightened ducks.

Pen hung on the landward rail. The port was in utter disarray. Five ships sunk at their moorings—Falun's galley now lay on its side, waterlogged—three still smoldering, the remains of one pier falling in blackened chunks into the water, a major segment of the waterfront burnt to the ground; really, the work the Orban fleet had come to do was already near-complete. With half its ships and captains out to sea, the Guild was in no position to offer resistance. They had apparently leapt on the offer of a negotiation.

While waiting for developments, Pen persuaded the aide to conduct the girls and himself on a tour of the war galley. Adelis had shown him around its fascinating complexity once before, a few months ago when it was in dock for winter maintenance in Vilnoc's navy yard, so not a few of the men recognized their general's Temple-man relative, compelling Pen to return salutes with a polite tally-sign and blessing. The rowers idling at their benches were military volunteers, no slaves here, and they and the soldiers seemed inclined to take Pen as more mascot than threat, along with his wards, who amused them. Although a number of the men, returning from a visit to the railing to study their erstwhile target of Lanti, cast him unsettled looks.

Adelis never believed in wasting time, so Penric was not too surprised to see him rowed back out to the *Eye of Orbas* at sunset. The faint Adelis-smirk on his face as he climbed back up the netting indicated the general was in a good mood, which seemed to hearten his welcoming men. Pen felt more cautious about that, but he didn't get an explanation till they were sitting down for dinner together.

Beneath a hooped canopy that sheltered a portion of the stern, illuminated by hanging lanterns, they perched cross-legged on cushions and were brought an onboard picnic, a cut above the lunch rations. The girls settled close at Pen's feet. Pen topped up Adelis's wine, not over-watered, and prodded him for his report from shore.

Adelis grinned and held his news hostage for Pen's tale first. Pen started with the dawn attack, though with a short doubling-back to complain of the archdivine of Trigonie whose delays had put Pen on that ship in the first place. He left out mentions of his brushes with the gods, though the bemused narrowing of Adelis's red-sparking eyes suggested he observed the lacunae. The collapses of Pen's first plan for ransom, and his second for the prison escape, he detailed but briefly; Pen thought it unnecessary of Adelis to laugh like a drain at the picture of Pen left swearing on the dock. Then a synopsis of their sojourn in the temple.

"Are you planning to attack Lanti Town?" Pen asked.

"Not at present," said Adelis.

"Because there are good people here as well as ill." Pen reflected on all he'd met, Jato, Godino, the friendly cook, the Mother's midwife, and on and on.

"The gods may be able to sort the just from the unjust soul by soul. I'm afraid armies must treat them in batches."

"Mm," Pen half-conceded. "I wonder if poor Godino remains safe. An attempt at rescue might just draw attention to him where there was none before."

"Possibly. If your Brother Godino is a man of sense he'll have taken to the hills by now."

"So I hope." Pen finished with the tersest description he could manage of his past day, which nonetheless made Adelis's eyebrows climb.

"You know, my offer to you to attend upon my army as an irregular auxiliary still stands," said Adelis, leadingly.

"And so does my refusal," Pen sighed.

It was an old argument. Adelis did not pursue it, turning instead to drawing more of their version of events from the Corva sisters. His efforts at kindliness were more labored than his Roknari, but the girls seemed to take them for sincere.

"The *parley*, Adelis," said Pen, when Adelis finished diverting himself with this.

"Ah, yes, that. I have wrangled a treaty from the Guild of Lantihera."

Pen blinked. "To what end?"

"An agreement to leave Orbas, its islands, and its shipping alone."

"Do you think they'll honor it?"

"For a season, perhaps. I've slipped a few agents ashore to watch for their inevitable lapse. Next time we can return in less of a scramble. Or, better, induce the Carpagamons to do so."

"You didn't look as if you were scrambling. Quite formidable."

"Learned, you have no idea what a miracle of logistics you observe before you. If it weren't for the sea maneuvers I'd talked Jurgo into, and which were supposed to take place next week, we wouldn't have sailed out of Vilnoc for another month."

"I daresay. So…a treaty in exchange for not invading Lantihera, which you weren't going to do in the first place?" No wonder Adelis had looked smug.

"I sweetened the pot by offering to not grant my fleet three days of shore leave."

"There's a difference between that and sacking the town?"

"Not much. The council took my point. You were a more fundamental bone of contention. To the tune of thirty thousand silver ryols."

Pen gasped, appalled. "That's a prince's ransom! Or, wait, no, were they demanding reparations…?"

Adelis stared, then laughed. "Ah, no, Penric! I wouldn't have offered a copper for that. No, that's what they're paying *us* to not leave you here."

Des crowed with delight.

Penric just…drank.

THE ORBAN fleet sailed on the morning tide, right after the coin chests were delivered.

Pen leaned on the stern rail with Adelis and watched the island recede behind them. That dwindling was the most desirable sight he could imagine.

"What will you do with my, my anti-ransom?" Pen asked him.

"It will be split. Part will be divided among my troops, to compensate them for the sad lack of loot from the sad lack of battle. The rest to Jurgo, to help pay for this sea-holiday."

"Maneuvers," corrected Pen. "Just a more realistic sort."

"That is an argument I will store up."

"Don't forget the share to the Temple."

"I'll leave that accounting to the duke."

Pen snickered. Sails raised, oars shipped, the breeze moved them for free, and in the right direction. White-and-gray harbor gulls swooped and shrieked in their wake, an unmelodic hymn to their recessional. The bold scavenger birds were considered creatures of the Bastard in these seas, he was reminded.

"It doesn't do any good, you know," Pen said at last. "All those ships and goods I destroyed were stolen in the first place. The Lanti pirates will just return to their trade with their efforts redoubled, to make up their losses."

"I expect so," said Adelis. "We could still turn back and raze the town." Pen was not entirely sure that was an idle jest. "Before they finish rebuilding that old Carpagamon fortress would actually be a good time."

Pen waved an averting hand. "I don't know what would stop the raiders altogether. The middle-merchants who buy the goods and people are as much a part of the system as the pirates, and the ones they sell them to even more so, and more diffuse and harder to attack. Being nearly everybody." Pen brooded. "The *cantons* manage without slavery."

"And are also very poor, you say."

"Mm." Pen could not altogether deny this. "Not that poor. We do well enough."

Adelis offered, "The Darthacans, I'm told, are building ships and warships off their far east coast that are all-sail, and don't require rowers. The rougher seas there have sunk more galleys than battles ever did, so that makes sense to me. If those designs do indeed prove superior, the time of galley slaves may come to an end without the need for virtuous canton austerity."

"But not in mines. Or the demand for concubines and servants." Scullions and scribes alike.

"I can't help you there. Not my trade. Pray to your gods, Learned."

"The gods take almost all who do not refuse them, slave or free. I'm not sure they see a difference between one form of human misery and another. They don't think the way we do. Soul by soul, as you say."

Adelis's black brows flicked up, perhaps at the disquiet of standing next to a man who could plausibly claim *any idea* of how the gods thought. "Thieves will still pursue other forms of treasure that they cannot otherwise earn, or just raid for mad bravado. And soldiers will still be called upon to put them down. I don't foresee an end to either of our trades in my lifetime."

"Nor mine, I suppose. Trade or lifetime." Pen turned to lean his back against the rail and study the Corva sisters, presently cross-legged on the other side of the stern being taught knots by a friendly sailor.

Adelis followed his glance, and asked with an odd diffidence, "Are those two god-touched, do you know?"

Because Pen could tell, being in an oblique chaotic sense god-touched himself?

Adelis went on, "They seem to have suffered the most extraordinary mix of chance and mischance, ill-luck and luck. Of which the most extraordinary was having you dropped atop them. Your god's white hand at work?"

"I wish I knew," sighed Pen. "Not one single thing that has happened requires an extraordinary explanation. It's just the, hm, accumulation." He pursed his lips. "I hope I get a chance to delve further into their mystery."

"If you do, pray share it." Adelis pushed off the rail, called away by some officer wanting his commander's attention. "If you can."

"Aye," said Penric.

Epilogue

AS MUCH AS Pen liked his upstairs study overlooking the shared well-court, he had to admit it grew close on a hot Vilnoc summer morning. So he'd moved the girls' language lesson down to the back pergola, its plank table and benches shaded by grape leaves, the surrounding pots of kitchen herbs lending a pleasantly rustic effect. The concentration of practicing Cedonian letters with slate and chalk had given way, in the languid warmth, to learning a few children's Temple hymns instead. Pen thought the rhythm, rhyme, and refrains did more, faster, to fix words in young brains than dry readings or recitations, not that the latter didn't have their place.

And he was able, without drudgery, to slip in the needed repetition by trying for harmony, his light baritone blending agreeably, he hoped, with the girls' sopranos. Curiously, Seuka's voice held to the key better than Lencia's; he fancied Lencia's busy mind was trying too hard. Still straining to be both lost mother and father to their truncated family, when being big sister seemed task enough to Pen.

Their rudimentary choir practice was interrupted by Nikys, rapping on a pergola support and smiling, so presumably not because she was being maddened by the noise. "Penric, we have a visitor."

He looked up and past her shoulder. The man hovering anxiously there was middle-aged, middle-sized, sturdy rather than stout. He wore ordinary dress of tunic, belt, and trousers, if well-made, and sensible sandals in this weather. His hair and beard were dark with a smattering of gray, his skin not Cedonian-brick but a paler warm tan that might have come from anywhere along the continent's more eastward coasts. Pen pegged it as Ibra by the familiar letter clutched tightly in his hand, and the girls' reactions.

"Papa!" shrieked Lencia; after an uncertain moment—it had been, what, over a year since they'd last seen the man—Seuka followed her bolt around the table.

He dropped to his knees and opened his arms to receive them, embracing them both at once, hard. "Ah," he huffed, dampening eyes closing in a grimace caught between joy and pain. In Ibran, he muttered, "Ah, so it's all true…"

"Master Ubi Getaf, I take it," said Pen, rising to greet this welcome, if sudden, apparition. The letter being abused in that thick fist was the one he'd written to Learned Iserne in Lodi, three weeks ago when they'd first reached Vilnoc, tightly summarizing his late adventures and begging her help in finding the wandering merchant. She had followed through splendidly, it seemed.

"Learned Penric?" said Getaf, less surely. He clambered to his feet and, both his hands being occupied by his clinging offspring, ducked his head at Penric. He continued in halting Cedonian, "I understand I have much to thank you for in rescuing my children."

Pen returned in smooth Ibran, "It was no more than any decent adult would have done, under the circumstances."

Well, perhaps a little *more,* murmured Des, amused. He would wait a while, Pen decided, to introduce Des.

Getaf's head went back as he parsed Pen's regional Ibran accent. "You…are from Brajar…?"

"No, but my language teacher was, long ago." *And I thank you for it, Learned Aulia*, he thought to that layer of Des that was the Brajaran Temple woman, who had once received Des from the dying Umelan like the baton in some mortal relay.

Getaf accepted this with another nod, too distracted to be curious. The girls dragged him to a bench, both trying to tell all their tale at once in a mixture of Roknari, which he seemed to speak well, and a little Ibran. He sat heavily, his head swinging back and forth like a man trying to follow some fast-moving ball game, or perhaps a bear befuddled by bees.

Nikys folded her arms and leaned back against the pergola post, listening in understandable bafflement, as she had some Roknari but no Ibran. But Pen thought she followed the emotions perfectly well, and approved. He pulled out his bench and motioned her to his side, where they sat, her soft thigh in its draped linen pressing companionably against his lean one. *Don't you dare disappear on me like that again* he received in a language more fundamental than any that tripped from his tongue. He grasped her plump hand and returned an equally silent, *Aye, Madame Owl.*

He murmured to her, "Does Getaf seem an upright fellow to you?"

Equally intent on the reunion playing out, Nikys murmured back, "Look at the girls. Such unhesitating gladness goes beyond just relief at a familiar face, I think."

Thanks in great part to Nikys the sisters were clean; shining hair neatly bound in braids and colored ties; fed, if not to sleekness, at least to the point that their natural skinniness no longer looked sunken with stress; and dressed in a superior grade of hand-me-downs that Nikys had begged from the duchess's household. Penric was pleased that they were able to present the pair to their papa in such good order, as though he were again a student offering some especially well-done work to one of his seminary masters. He hoped he'd get a good mark.

Getaf's expression sobered as the girls worked their way back to the tale of their mother's death, the details all new to him since Pen's letter had devoted only a clause about *died from illness in Raspay* to the root calamity.

"I am so sorry," he told them. "I'd heard nothing of this. When the prince of Jokona's border clash with Ibra closed his coasts to Zagosur trade, I thought to wait it out with a venture west. The Zagosur factor should have forwarded your letter to me, not returned it. And Taspeig should most certainly have accompanied you all the way to Lodi, not abandoned you at Agenno, although...although that might not have helped."

"She was very tired and cranky by then," Lencia offered in excuse. "We all were. And I think she was running out of money."

"Still. Still."

Seuka raised her face. "Are you going to take us home now, Papa?"

Getaf hesitated, too palpably. Where was home for these sisters now, really? Raspay seemed as abandoned behind them as any sunken ship, with not even a floating spar left to cling to.

Lencia, as ever the more alert to the difficulties, put in, "Or at least take us along with you?"

That was a, hm, not-bad picture, of living like young apprentices trailing a master trader and learning the world, as many such men made their sons. And sometimes daughters.

Getaf rubbed his forehead, frowning into his lap. "That presents certain problems, which I must take thought for. I can't take you back to Zagosur. Which, I suppose, was never home for you anyway. But I won't leave you without succor; that, I promise." He looked across at Pen and switched to Cedonian. "Learned Penric, may I speak with you in private for a moment?"

Pen and Nikys glanced at each other. Nikys rose, and said kindly, "Lencia, Seuka, can you come help me fetch food and drink for your papa?"

Lencia frowned, and Seuka's lower lip stuck out, wary of the risk of people arranging their lives without their say-so. Penric sympathized, but construed there might be personal matters Getaf didn't wish to share with them. As well, Nikys could seize this chance for a candid conference with his daughters. Pen nodded brightly at them, and they let themselves be shuffled off, only dragging their sandaled feet a little.

Getaf watched them disappear into the house, then lowered his voice and said in Ibran, "May I take it they were not worse abused by the pirates?"

"You may. Apparently due to their higher sale value as virgins. Which, er, they have retained."

Getaf nodded in relief. Then paused, mustering his words. "Your friend Learned Iserne caught up with me just in time in Lodi. I'd finished amassing my trade goods there, and in another week I would have been on my way back to Zagosur." He chewed his lip. "I don't think it wise to try to take Lencia and Seuka to my household there. My wife holds all in firm hands, very reliable manager, has nurtured our own children near to maturity, with a useful web of in-laws, but... I don't think she would make them very welcome. They deserve better than grudging care, and because of my business I would not be much there to provide a balancing weight."

"I gather Madame Getaf does not know about your mistress?" Or had Jedula Corva been more in the nature of a second wife?

Getaf shook his head. "And I'd prefer to keep it that way. Given there is nothing left in Raspay to argue about."

"Understandable..."

"Jedula was an anchor to me, but to the extent I'd thought about anything happening to her and not me, I assumed I would pay Taspeig to care for the girls, in their house as before. I can't see taking them back to Taspeig now, given her unreliable behavior in Agenno. Anyway, I expect she has gone on to find some other life for herself. And the status of half-Quintarian orphans in Raspay, even if they're not destitute, is not happy."

"So I've heard."

Getaf stared into his hands, cradled between his knees, then looked up at Pen more keenly. "What can you tell me about the Bastard's Order here in Vilnoc? Is it well-run?"

Pen's brows rose. "The orphanage is as decent as it can manage. Chronically short of funds and staff, like most such places, but its people are very dedicated."

Getaf waved this aside. "No, no. I'd take our chances in Zagosur before I'd leave the girls in an orphanage. Spare those resources for the truly needy. I'm thinking about the chapterhouse itself. Lencia and especially Seuka are a little young to be placed as dowered dedicats to the Order, but... perhaps you have some influence there?"

"Huh." Pen folded his arms on the plank table. "There's an interesting notion."

"A good chapterhouse might assume their care and education at a higher level than an orphanage can provide, and keep them together if their dower-contract so instructed. And…and for the first time in their lives, their birth-status might make them more, not less, welcomed. Um—where have they been staying in Vilnoc till now? Your letter was unclear on that point." He pressed the wrinkled paper out on the table in a nervous gesture.

"Oh, sorry. They've been staying here. I suppose you can think of my house as a branch of the Order, irregular senior member as I am."

Getaf looked up in hesitation. "Do you think you…? Would your wife…?"

Pen felt his way forward, sharing Getaf's uncertainty. Nikys had been nothing but generous to the lost girls, but was it right to pledge her labor into an indefinite future when a perfectly good parent had turned up after all, willing to do his part? Even more central, what was the optimum opportunity for Lencia and Seuka?

"I…actually think the chapterhouse would make a better regular domicile for them," Pen said slowly, "given the erratic nature of my own duties, and also those of Nikys and Adelis. And there would be more kinds of people around to teach and train them, not to mention a supply of energetic young fellow-dedicats to befriend. But, really, this need not be either-or. It's only a short walk from here. Looking in on each other would be an easy task."

Lord Bastard, is this your intent? Pen would pray to his god for guidance, but he never did get any back when he did that, so he supposed he must use his own judgment. Though capturing two such bright souls for His Order must surely be an acceptable offering.

Getaf said wistfully, "Do they seem to like Vilnoc?"

"So far as I can tell. Though any place must seem better than Lantihera, or whatever slavery would have followed."

A wry, conceding nod. "I could make sure my travels extend toward Lodi again. And visit, from time to time." Left unspoken were the hazards of his own trade—Pen was put in mind of Aloro and Arditi, and hoped they'd made it back alive to Adria.

"Well, then, I suggest you put the proposal to your daughters, and discover what they think of it. I see no impediment from this end."

Getaf's stiff shoulders eased at this reassurance. "It could be well. It might be very well."

"It might." Pen pulled his queue around—Seuka had insisted on her turn to braid, this morning—and fiddled with it, perhaps not concealing his nosiness as much as he'd wish. "Do you think their mother would approve?"

An aching sort of shrug at this reminder of grief. "I can only pray so. But if they flourish, then yes. It was all she ever wanted for her girls, their well-being."

"How did you two come to meet?" Which wasn't really the question. But *How did you two come to form a bond that could not even be broken by death?* seemed too intimate a query for an hour's acquaintance.

A brief smile. "Through her work, of course. When I was first trying to set up trade in Raspay, what, fifteen years ago now. I moved from being her regular client to her exclusive client whenever I prospered enough for it, which…wasn't all the time, to my frustration. But we made do. Sometimes, she was my temporary factor, when I could afford no other assistance."

Which also sounded far more like a merchant's wife than his mistress. Well, apart from her side-jobs.

"Was she very young and beautiful, back then?"

Getaf waved an indifferent hand. "Only a little younger than me—granted, I was younger then, too. Well-looking enough, as one must be for her trade. But she made the best of herself through tidiness and health, not by the unearned gift that's the blessing and curse of those born beautiful." He flicked a shrewd glance at Pen, which Pen pretended not to notice.

Getaf's expression softened. "But she was the most endlessly kind person I have ever met, of any sex or sort. Her fearless caring terrified me at times. She would take in strays, you know, others of her profession who had run into rotten situations of one sort and another. Especially the young ones, who had grown no slyness or deceit by which to defend themselves. I lost count of the number of secret Quintarians and ill-treated whores and crow-lads I smuggled out of Raspay with me as servants, to release in some port of Ibra in the hopes they might find a safer life. A few escaped Quintarian slaves, too—now, that was a dangerous game all around. I much preferred to just buy out the battered ones at Jedula's direction, when I could afford it. Better for my poor heart."

Penric blinked at this new picture. "Did Lencia and Seuka know all this was going on?"

"I don't think so, or only the tip of it, when Jedula hid someone sick or injured in our house.

She would certainly have misdirected or sworn the girls to silence, in those cases. But for the most part she took great care to keep them ignorant of those activities. Because even as shunned as they were in Raspay, they still had a few young friends, if only the children of others in their mother's trade. And there would have been no controlling their chatter."

"I see."

Oh, my, agreed Des.

For the first time, the hidden bud of Jedula Corva's relationship with her god seemed to unfold its secrets before Pen's eye like a blooming flower. Beloved, god-touched, great-souled…a saint, even? The true sort, who moved through the world as silently as fishes, unnoticed by carnal eyes that focused only on outward domination and display. Never on a small woman in a small town, being *kind*. Soul by soul.

And her faithful lieutenant, it seemed. Pen studied the unprepossessing, middle-aged merchant, sitting oblivious to these reflections, anew.

Getaf sighed. "I suppose Jedula spoiled me for any other woman. Any other person, really. My life is going to be much…duller, now." His grimace didn't much resemble the buffering smile he evidently intended.

God-touched at least, then. Pen recognized that particular bereft longing left when a great Presence became a great absence. That heartbroken loss only known to those who, at some perilous apogee, had *almost* grasped that inchoate, indescribable essence.

The gods make it up to us at the end, I suppose. For some, that was a long and tedious wait.

A bustle at the house door; Nikys and the girls bearing trays of cool lemon-water and tasty pastries. Pen amazed the company and amused himself by generating balls of ice for their drinks. He also took this peaceable opportunity to introduce Des; they were successful at not disturbing his visitor too much. The diversion gave time to settle his own upended mind, anyway.

Getaf, who was, Pen mused, a successful trader and therefore negotiator, pitched his proposal to his daughters over the meal. Pen tried to maintain a neutral mien while this was going on, but he supposed his broad smile betrayed him when the girls leaped on his invitation to give the family a personal tour of the chapterhouse that afternoon, to examine what they were being offered more closely. Getaf definitely approved of that mercantile due diligence. Even when the sisters' caginess was a transparent effort not to sadden him by appearing too eager to leave his protection.

THE AGREEMENT between an Order and the parents or guardians of a young dedicat fell somewhere between a dower and an apprenticeship; Getaf, apparently experienced with both sorts of contracts, ironed out the details with the Bastard's chapterhouse within two days. Waiving the age requirements, upon examination of the matter by the chapter head, was routine enough to scarcely need Pen's clout. Children so placed would, upon their majority, have the choice of regularizing their oaths to full membership, or leaving for a lay life. Pen had no idea which Lencia and Seuka would then choose, and finally decided it was not his task to guess so many years ahead.

Good, said Des. *You borrow enough trouble already you'd need a counting-house to keep your ledger.*

Pen, Nikys, and Getaf together escorted the sisters to their new home. The girls had taken to Nikys— as who would not?—and Nikys to them reciprocally. They all helped haul their few belongings through the chapterhouse's back courtyard up to their narrow room, which had a glassed casement overlooking the town and the valley that wound up into the hills behind it. Also a wardrobe, a pair of chests, a washstand with its paraphernalia, an inviting book-shelf—Pen approved—and two beds, one on either side; Seuka promptly sat and bounced on hers, con-sideringly. Lencia stared around in both curiosity and trepidation, but Pen fancied the first was winning.

Then it was time to see Getaf off in turn. The man was plainly torn between concern for Lencia and Seuka, and worrying about what might be hap-pening to his year's worth of work waiting in a Lodi warehouse. And Jedula Corva's daughters, Pen was reminded, were not Getaf's only children that he had left to hope and the care of others while he journeyed, though he tactfully did not speak much of his other family in Zagosur.

It was a short walk from the chapterhouse to Vilnoc's harbor. The skies had regained the deep blue of summer, and the gulls flashed almost pain-fully white against it. There were hugs, there were tears, there were probably futile admonishments against the risks of life in Vilnoc and on ships. Then the merchant pressed his coin into the hand of the oarsman and was rowed out to his waiting vessel.

Getaf climbed the net and waved one last time before the crew urged him out of their way.

"Will he be safe?" fretted Seuka. All too aware, now, not just of the hazards of the world, but of the fragility of grownups.

"The storm season is over in these waters," said Penric. "And I don't think pirates will be attacking ships under Orban flags again so soon. He's as safe as anyone alive and moving in the world can be."

Nikys put in, "We can stop at the Vilnoc temple and pray for him, if you like."

Lencia looked down at her sandals, up at Penric. "Does it help?"

"For a certainty…only at the very end of all journeys," said Penric, his god-sworn honesty wrestling down more soothing platitudes. "But at least there we don't travel alone."

Lencia, after a sober moment, nodded.

They turned into the city's streets. Bumping companionably between Penric, Des, and Nikys, the Corva sisters climbed undaunted.